For Ronald Martin Solan
Artist, soldier, Porter Street irregular

Copyright © 2015 by Scholastic Inc.

All rights reserved. Published by Scholastic Inc., *Publishers since 1920.*
SCHOLASTIC, TOMBQUEST, and associated logos are trademarks and/or
registered trademarks of Scholastic Inc.

Library of Congress Control Number: 2014959843

ISBN 978-0-545-72340-4

10 9 8 7 6 5 4 3 2   15 16 17 18 19/0

Printed in the U.S.A. 23
First edition, August 2015
Book design by Keirsten Geise

Scholastic US: 557 Broadway · New York, NY 10012
Scholastic Canada: 604 King Street West · Toronto, ON M5V 1E1
Scholastic New Zealand Limited: Private Bag 94407 · Greenmount, Manukau 2141
Scholastic UK Ltd.: Euston House · 24 Eversholt Street · London NW1 1DB

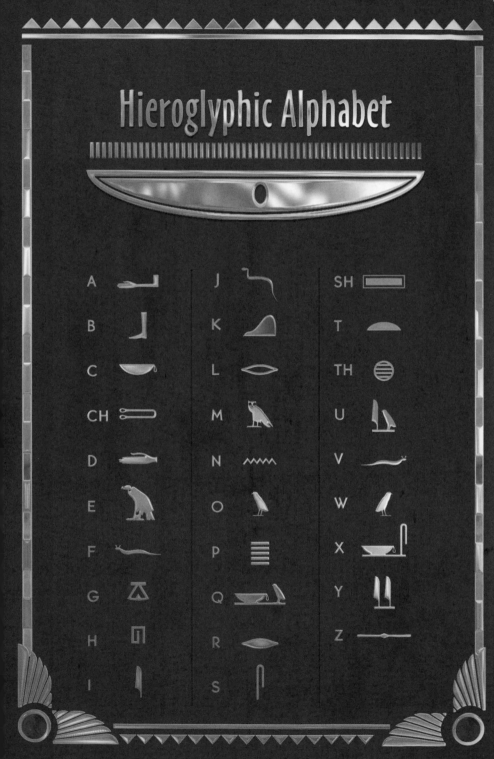

Hieroglyphic Alphabet

A		J		SH	
B		K		T	
C		L		TH	
CH		M		U	
D		N		V	
E		O		W	
F		P		X	
G		Q		Y	
H		R		Z	
I		S			

TOMBQUEST
VALLEY OF KINGS

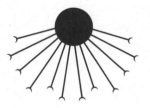

MICHAEL NORTHROP

SCHOLASTIC INC.

Hungry Ghosts

His name was Abdel. Once, he had been Mr. Shahin, the boss of ten men. But like so many in Cairo, he had fallen on hard times. Now, he was a proud man in a cheap suit — a good man in bad company. Desperation had brought him here, but he was worried.

"What's this job you have for me?" he said, trying hard to hold his voice steady.

The towering man next to him answered with the same three words as last time: "You will see."

Abdel glanced over at him. Was this man truly the leader of The Order, the criminal cult that had haunted Egypt for thousands of years? He certainly looked the part, tall and strong and wearing a suit more expensive than Abdel's car. Under his arm was a large, elegant leather bag.

"Nothing illegal," Abdel added. "You promised me . . ."

"Of course not," said the man, a hint of amusement slipping into his flat, cold voice. "As I said, you are here to help."

Abdel nodded, forcing himself to think of the food he would buy his family, maybe even long-overdue birthday gifts for his children. Still, he wondered what sort of help he could offer in a drafty warehouse on the edge of the city.

Their footsteps echoed in the massive space as they approached a heavy steel door. "Here we are," said the cult leader.

Abdel eyed the thick bar holding the door closed as the man slipped the bag from under his arm and began unzipping it. "You will excuse my new appearance," he said, removing a heavy golden mask and letting the bag fall to the floor. "But as you know, we are a very old organization, and we have certain . . . traditions."

Abdel had hoped those "traditions" were rumors or exaggerations, but now he knew better. He gaped at the mask. It was an Egyptian vulture made of finely wrought gold, showing every fold and pockmark of the vulture's skin. The beak was forged of sharp iron. The leader slipped it on carefully, and his words echoed out from underneath: "Open the door!"

Abdel suddenly understood that he had made a deal with the devil. He knew that he should refuse, that he should *run*. And yet the powerful voice thundered in his head, robbed him of his will. With fear-widened eyes, he watched his own hand pull the handle of the bar up and back. The door began to rattle against its hinges, and fresh voices reached his ears. A chorus of sinister whispers buzzed around him, and his warm skin went cold.

The bar slid aside with a loud *thunk*.

Suddenly, the door opened inward, releasing a rush of

stinking air and a swarm of dark whispers so strong that Abdel could feel them, like snake tongues on his skin. And for a moment — one brief, horrible moment — he saw it.

An abomination.

"That . . . should not . . . be," he managed.

Two powerful hands pushed him, strong palms slapping his back. "Ooof!" he gasped as he stumbled forward into the room. The door slammed shut behind him, and in the sudden darkness, he heard the bar slide shut.

Ten thousand whispers combined into one word — "Welcome" — before shattering back into pieces. Unleashed, the heavy whispers cut into him, no longer tongues but teeth! Each one grabbed a piece, tore it off, gobbled it down. It wasn't his body they were devouring; it was his soul. The effect was the same. His pulse revved for a moment from fear and pain.

And then it thickened.

And slowed.

And, finally, it stopped.

What was left of his soul slipped free of his body and was torn to bits, devoured.

Abdel Shahin was a good man, and that was what they liked.

$\longleftarrow\!\!+\!\!-\!\!+\!\!-\!\!+\!\!\longrightarrow$

Elsewhere in the old warehouse, a second man emerged from the shadows. He had kept his distance during the feeding and now cast a nervous look at the barred door. Little more than a ridiculous decoration, he knew. What was inside could not be contained. In a sense, it was already loose.

The man pried his eyes from the door. "We have received information from the source," he said.

"Have the amulet keepers arrived?" said the leader, carefully placing the heavy mask back in its leather carrier.

"Yes," said the man. "They are here."

"And Peshwar awaits them?" said the leader.

The man hesitated. "Yes, but . . . are you sure this is the right way? If we give them more time, if we follow them . . . they could lead us to the Spells."

"No," said the leader flatly, "they have troubled us enough. We will cut them down. Leave the others in a ditch, but bring me the boy. Whatever he knows of his mother we will wring from him."

The man nodded. Challenging the leader on anything was dangerous. Challenging him about the boy could be suicide. "I have told Peshwar this, but she has no mercy in her. I worry she will kill them all, and whatever they know will die with them."

"Then tell her to think of it as playing with her prey," said the leader, zipping up the bag. "Cats are good at that."

Voices of the Dead

The thin metal skin of a battered taxi was all that stood between Alex Sennefer and a city at war with itself. The car wove its way through madhouse Cairo traffic as news reports on the radio screamed of a crime wave for the ages. But as the cab sped past groups of heavily armed police, Alex thought they seemed to be huddled together less to protect the public than themselves.

He glanced around the cab at his own compatriots. His athletic older cousin, Luke, sat next to him, dressed as if for basketball, and Alex's best friend, Renata Duran, was barely visible on Luke's opposite side. In the front seat were the mysterious scholar Dr. Ernst Todtman and the taxi driver, who leaned heavily on his horn.

Alex flinched from the noise. His nerves were shot and his thoughts were dark. He tried to shut out the chaos of Egypt's capital as he remembered his time in England. Once again, he saw a man in a fearsome mask shouting questions at him in the eerie tomb beneath Highgate

Cemetery. *"Where is your mother, little boy?"* He remembered the words so clearly that the man could have been in the taxi with him.

But of course, if he had been, one of them would be dead by now. The man was Ta-mesah, a top lieutenant of The Order. The mask was a powerful artifact in the shape of a crocodile's head and capable, Alex knew from firsthand experience, of inflicting tremendous pain. *"She must be in the Black Land,"* Ta-mesah had shouted. *"Tell us where!"*

And now Alex was in the Black Land — Egypt, named for the rich, dark soil on the banks of the Nile River.

Those words had changed everything. Before them, Alex had believed that The Order had kidnapped his mom. That they'd taken her and also stolen the Lost Spells of the Egyptian Book of the Dead from the Metropolitan Museum of Art in New York. But after Ta-mesah's words, he knew the ancient cult didn't have her — that they were hunting for her, too. Now Alex and The Order were in a race to find her, and with her, perhaps, the Spells.

His mom had used the massive power of the Spells to bring Alex back from the brink of death. But in doing so, she had accidentally opened a gateway to the afterlife and released the evil ancients known as the Death Walkers. Now those sinister beings were working with The Order toward some dark end Alex could only guess at.

All this evil unleashed just to save his life. He felt a familiar wave of guilt at the thought, both a weight on his shoulders and a punch in his gut.

The traffic began to slow down, and the taxi's air conditioning gave out with one last, dying wheeze. The driver shouted something in Arabic and pressed the button to lower the windows. Warm air hit Alex in the face. It wasn't so bad while they were moving, but a moment later they ground to a full halt. A toxic mix of smells settled into the still air: uncollected trash from the curb, sulfurous fumes from the traffic, and the heavy smog that hung over the city.

"Ugh," said Luke, burying his face in his hands.

"Did you know," Ren began, leaning over to raise her window back up. Alex smiled despite the stench: *Did you know* were three of his friend's favorite words. Ren continued: ". . . that living in Cairo is the same as smoking a pack of cigarettes a day?"

Alex flicked his eyes out over the city. The day was ending now and the sky was doubly clouded by weak light and strong smog. The buildings faded into a gray haze in the distance.

"It is not just the air that is bad here now," added the driver in heavily accented English. "The whole city has gone mad."

Alex's eyes were beginning to water from the combination of odors. As he reached down to pull his T-shirt up over his nose and mouth, he heard shouting from the sidewalk. He turned his head in time to see a woman run headlong into the front window of a small store. The woman tumbled inside under a razor-sharp shower of broken glass.

"Is she hurt?" blurted Ren at the exact same moment that Luke said, "That was crazy!"

The taxi began moving again as the traffic crept forward. Alex kept his eyes on the shattered window as it disappeared behind them, looking for movement inside the store's shadowy interior.

"Why would she do that?" he said to no one in particular.

It was the taxi driver who answered. "They say the voices of the dead haunt the city now," he said. "Carried on the wind. Telling truth, telling lies, it doesn't matter. They sow anger and seek to harm."

"Yeah, but that was seriously bazonkers," said Luke.

The driver paused, possibly trying to figure out what *bazonkers* meant. "That," he said finally, "was nothing."

His tone suggested that he was done with the subject, but Todtman wasn't going to let it go. "What have you seen?" he asked.

The driver paused, considering it, then took a deep breath and answered. "I was at the hospital last night. My wife had been stabbed." Alex heard Ren draw in a sharp breath.

"I am sorry," said Todtman, but the driver shook him off. Now that he had started, he seemed determined to tell the story.

"She will recover," he said. "But the hospital was like a war zone, and we left before we could see the doctor. We didn't trust him."

"Why not?" said Todtman, continuing his gentle prodding.

"Because he had attacked the previous patient with a metal crutch. It was late, you see" — he paused once more to weigh his words — "and the voices are worse at night."

Alex looked out his window at the darkening sky above them and felt a shudder of fear run through him.

The taxi pulled off to the side of the road and came to one final abrupt halt.

"We are here," said the driver. "Good luck."

|||

Back Against the Wall

Alex slid across the seat and exited curbside, and the friends dragged their bags toward a large apartment complex. Ren and Todtman rolled prim wheelie bags, while Alex and Luke lugged heavy suitcases.

Todtman was in the lead, slowed down only slightly by a noticeable limp. Alex could follow the old scholar by sound alone — the hum of his wheelie bag and the steady click-clack of his black walking stick — so he let his eyes wander. The city was alien and dangerous, but he was looking for something much more familiar: his mom.

He knew it was crazy to think he'd spot her in a city of millions. But then, craziness was all around him now. Everyone thought she was in Egypt, and this was the capital, a few blocks away from the largest collection of Egyptian artifacts on the planet. Before she'd used the Lost Spells to heal him, Alex had always been too sick or weak to travel with her when she came here for work. Instead, she'd described the streets of Cairo and the wonders they led to, telling him true stories that felt like fairy tales. *What better place for a missing Egyptologist?* he thought.

He saw a woman with brown hair like his mom's and nearly gave himself whiplash turning to look. *Nothing. Not her.*

He checked to see if Ren had seen him acting crazy, but she was looking at the buildings, sizing up the angles and architecture. She got that from her dad, a senior engineer who'd worked alongside his mom back at the Metropolitan Museum of Art.

Ponytail! Pantsuit! His head whipped around again. Not her.

He glanced up at the apartment complex. A tall brick wall surrounded it, and Todtman was leading them toward the lone opening in the center. This was where they were supposed to stay. The rooms had been arranged by Todtman's contact at the Supreme Council of Antiquities, the powerful agency in charge of Egypt's ancient treasures.

Alex forced himself to stop scanning the sidewalk for his mom and tried to focus. *We have other fish to fry*, he told himself, but even that phrase came from her — and reminded him of what a bad cook she was. "What is it?" he'd ask her when presented with her latest on-the-fly concoction. "Burned," she'd answer, an inside joke but often true.

Maybe she'll *be the one to find* me, he thought, but that really was crazy. If she wanted to find him, all she had to do was call. *So why doesn't she?* he thought for the one-millionth time. He looked down at his phone. Nothing. If she was really out there — if she really had the Lost Spells, like everyone seemed to think — why didn't she call and tell him where she was? *She must have a reason*, he told himself. *But what?* He was so distracted he didn't notice that the click-clacking of Todtman's cane had stopped — until he walked right into the German's back.

"Sorry," said Alex, retreating — right into Ren.

"Hey!" she said.

"What's up?" said Luke, smoothly sidestepping the jumbled bodies.

Todtman pushed his palm toward the ground — *quiet, please* — and then waved them all to the side. "Over here!" he whispered urgently, motioning them toward the brick wall on one side of the entrance.

Alex knew it was serious when Todtman lifted his bag's wheels off the ground and didn't use his cane, choosing to limp quietly — and painfully — over. The others huddled up against the wall next to him.

"I don't think she saw us," said Dr. Todtman, nodding toward some unseen enemy inside the complex. His face was always a little froggy, with eyes that protruded too much and a chin that protruded too little, but fear now amplified the effect.

"Who?" said Alex, resting his suitcase on the ground.

"So we're not going in?" said Luke, a little too loud. He was fast on his feet but could be painfully slow on the uptake.

The other three shushed him.

"Peshwar," said Todtman, as if it were the name of a particularly gruesome disease. "She is another Order operative. And it seems she is waiting for us."

Alex flattened back against the wall. The bricks were still radiating heat left over from the blazing Egyptian day but Todtman's words sent a chill through him. *How did she know we were coming?*

"We can't stay here," said Todtman.

Alex glanced up at the sky — as dark as gray wool now — and the taxi driver's words came back to him: *"The voices are worse at night."*

"We will have to make other arrangements," said Todtman. "I have a friend here . . . It has been years, but maybe . . ."

Suddenly, Alex heard footsteps coming from the other side of the wall: the brisk slap of expensive shoes on the stone walkway. Alex pushed himself off the wall. Instinctively, his left hand reached up and wrapped around the ancient scarab amulet that hung from a chain beneath his shirt. He felt his pulse rev and his mind calm as the magic of the ancient amulet surged through him.

A man in a tan, summer-weight suit walked out through the entryway in the wall and turned toward them. His cold eyes lit up with recognition.

"Walak!" he shouted in Arabic, before turning and waving to whoever was behind him. He was an Order thug, calling for backup.

Alex gripped his amulet tighter with his left hand as his

right shot up and unleashed a spear of concentrated wind that knocked the man back against the wall.

"Kuhh!" he said as his head hit the bricks and his eyes fluttered closed.

But as fast as Alex had acted, it wasn't fast enough.

More footsteps sounded from inside the complex. A stampede of Order muscle was heading toward them!

"Let's go!" said Ren.

Luke, an elite athlete with Olympic dreams, leaned forward into a sprinter's stance. But Alex knew that they weren't running anywhere. Todtman's left leg had been crippled by a scorpion sting back in New York. He looked over to see Todtman's own amulet, a jewel-eyed falcon known as the Watcher, disappear into the scholar's hand.

"Ahlan!" he shouted.

It was one of the few Arabic words Alex knew, a simple greeting. Several pedestrians who'd stopped to gawk at the fallen thug now looked over at Todtman and snapped to attention. They immediately rushed into the opening in the wall, forming a tightly shut human gate. The Watcher could do more than watch . . .

"This way! Leave the bags!" said Todtman, his cane already clacking down the sidewalk.

Alex looked over at the people blocking the opening in the wall. They were a tangled mass of intertwined arms and legs, but he saw other arms now, other hands. The Order's thugs were already pushing their way through.

And then a flash of crimson light lit the Egyptian dusk and people began to fall to the ground.

"Over here!" called Todtman, cutting through a double strand of police tape with a swipe of his cane and turning down a side alley.

They'd come to Egypt to battle the Death Walkers and to find the Lost Spells and, hopefully, Alex's mom. But once again, they were the ones being hunted.

Alex hustled down the alley alongside Ren. Todtman was half a limp ahead, and Luke had fallen back to serve as rear guard.

Ren gave Alex a quick look: *Here we go again.*

Her own amulet, an ibis she'd been given deep under that London cemetery, bounced at her neck. Unlike him, she hadn't reached for it once during the encounter. He knew she still didn't trust it — or the magic that powered it — but he wished she would. Because it could provide the one thing they needed most: answers.

As the sky above them darkened, the alleyway behind them lit up a brilliant red. A scream split the air like a knife.

Footsteps. Voices.

"I can't outrun them," said Todtman, grimacing with every rushed step on his injured leg as they turned onto a broader service alley behind a row of apartment buildings.

"I can help," said Ren, rushing up to Todtman. At not quite four-and-a-half feet tall, she was essentially crutch-sized.

But Todtman had a different strategy in mind. He lifted his cane and pointed toward a small garage, its roll-down metal door halfway open. "We'll take cover in there," he said.

"There?" said Ren skeptically.

Alex looked at the slice of deep darkness inside, but it wasn't the possibility of spiders or scorpions or last week's trash inside that worried him. It was the possibility of trapping themselves.

Suddenly, he heard voices in the side alley they'd just come from. Their pursuers had picked up their trail again.

"Hurry!" said Todtman, once again limping over without his cane to avoid its noisy beat.

He ducked stiffly under the roll-gate, and the others filed

in after him like a line of ducklings. Alex crouched down in the gray light of the service alley and straightened up into darkness. His first whiff of the air inside told him he'd been right about the garbage.

"We need to close this," said Todtman.

Luke was already leaning into it. "Stuck," he grunted. "Stuck bad."

"Step back, please," said Todtman. "Alex?"

Alex reached up, wrapped his left hand around his amulet, and felt the electric thrill of its power surge through his system. A few feet away, Todtman did the same.

"Go," whispered Todtman.

Alex lifted his right hand, spread his fingers, and then pushed them slowly toward the ground. One side of the door was farther down. *The other side is jammed*, thought Alex, and he concentrated on that one. The old gate groaned in response but did little more than shift and shiver.

"More," said Todtman.

Alex pushed harder. Todtman must have, too, because suddenly the gate snapped shut with a loud metallic rumble.

Way too loud! thought Alex.

If The Order had already made the turn into the service alley, then the friends had just closed the lid on their own coffin.

Everyone held their breath.

Alex risked a few whispered words: "Ren, use your amulet. Can you see anything?"

No response.

In the darkness of their pungent sardine can, he couldn't tell if she was ignoring him or already holding her mysterious ibis, trying to puzzle out whatever image it gave her.

He heard footsteps. Voices.

The sounds came through the gate so clearly — conducted by the metal — that Alex briefly wondered if they could hear his own hammering heartbeat on the other side.

"It sounds like they knocked something over," said one of the thugs. "Check the ground."

Alex tried to count the footsteps. *How many of them were there?* Then a new voice stopped him cold.

"The German will try to cloud your mind." It was a woman's voice, dry and scratchy, as desolate as a desert wind. "Do not look him in the eyes. Shoot him first."

Guns. The Order thugs had only carried knives in London. *They don't fear the law here*, he realized. *We're on their turf, and they fear nothing.*

Alex heard a faint sound coming from somewhere behind the garage, like raindrops or soft footsteps.

"Wait!" It was a man's voice, directly outside.

Alex stiffened. He pictured the metal gate flying up and bullets filling the darkness. His amulet could do amazing things, but he had no illusions that it could stop bullets. A sense of hopelessness filled him. A sudden fear that his mom would never know what happened to him — and he would never know what happened to her.

Another sound, farther off, like a single loud hand-clap.

"That door!" said the same man. "Someone just closed it!"

Footsteps again, this time hard and heading away.

"This way," hissed Todtman. Weak light flooded in, a gray rectangle appearing in the wall as the doctor opened a side door. "Quickly," he whispered. "It won't take them long to realize their mistake."

There was commotion behind them as the door that had just been closed was broken down. Wood splintered, and Alex turned just in time to see the last figure in line glide silently into the house: a very thin woman wearing a pale white mask — the skull of a lioness. A shiver went through him. Peshwar.

As she disappeared inside, the doorway lit up red. The Order had followed the wrong trail and someone else had just paid the price.

Todtman led them to the end of the alley. He didn't risk using his cane until they made a quick turn onto a side street. Farther from the big buildings of the main avenues, the city changed. Houses were smaller and closer together; everything was concrete or brick in shades of gray or brown or tan. Mangy-looking stray dogs picked at scattered garbage piles. One of the stray dogs started following them, and not in a friendly way. Its fur was matted and stained, white foam dripping ominously from its mouth.

Here and there, tantalizing scents of strong spices and simmering food wafted out of open windows. But so too did loud, angry arguments. Emergency sirens echoed down the narrow streets.

The twilight settled around them like a gray shawl, the first streetlights just now blinking on. To Alex, this was scarier than total darkness. At least you could hide in darkness. "What happened back there?" he said.

"Someone picked the wrong time to take out the trash," said Ren.

"They almost added us to the pile," said Luke. "They had guns and maybe like a laser or something. They were going to go full-on Call of Duty on us!"

"That wasn't a laser," said Alex.

Luke looked at him and then glanced down at Alex's scarab beetle amulet as it reflected the soft glow of a streetlight. Luke made the connection. "All right, bug boy, a magic laser — a maser. I don't want to get hit by it either way —"

There was a low growl right behind them. They looked back. The mangy dog was closer now. As it crossed under the streetlight, the white foam around its mouth seemed to glow. Todtman led them away, onto another side street.

"Do you think we lost Peshwar?" Alex asked.

"We will not lose her until her hunt is over," he said. "One way or the other."

A few blocks later, Todtman came to a stop outside an abandoned three-story building. Its windows were boarded up or painted over, and the front door was layered with notices from the city: CONDEMNED.

"Uh, guys?" said Ren. The dog had appeared again behind them, circling toward Ren: the smallest target. Alex instinctively stepped between her and the filthy hound. It was close now, one quick lunge and snap away. He didn't want to hurt the thing but . . . His hand slid up toward his scarab as he looked back toward Todtman, standing by the door.

"How do we get in?" said Alex. "There's not even a doorbell."

"Not as such," said Todtman, reaching up and wrapping his hand around his amulet.

Almost immediately, Alex heard movement inside.

A voice came through the doorway, and the stray dog cocked its head. *Memories of some long-lost home*, Alex thought, and his hand fell away from his amulet. *Poor thing.*

Sirens wailed in the distance; somewhere, a gunshot.

The door opened, and the rabid dog slunk away.

Shangri-la

The door swung shut behind them with a thick *THUNK*. The man who'd slammed it exhaled, clearly relieved to have the chaos of Cairo shut out once more.

"Hello, I'm Jinn," he said, a thick Egyptian accent decorating his seamless English. "Of course, that's not my real name. And this is my little urban Shangri-la." He gestured at the large, dimly lit room. "I steal the electricity."

Alex looked around. The place seemed to be from another world — or at least another time. He wasn't surprised to see all the ancient Egyptian touches — this was a colleague of Todtman's after all, and they were in Egypt. He'd just never seen these kinds of ancient treasures look so . . . lived in. The leaves of a houseplant spilled out of an alabaster bowl that had to be at least two thousand years old. A square of tattered, hieroglyph-covered cloth hung on the wall like a poster for a rock band.

"Nice stuff," said Luke. "Any way we could get *our* things back?"

Todtman chuckled softly. "Our bags have been taken and sold by now. We can buy new supplies tomorrow."

"Let me show you to your rooms upstairs," said Jinn.

"Great," said Luke. "I can put all of my nonexistent stuff away."

There was a scuttling sound above them. Alex, Ren, and Luke all froze and looked up at the ceiling.

"Are there other people here?" said Ren, her shoulders tensing.

"Yes," said Jinn.

Ren relaxed a little.

"But I'm pretty sure those were rats."

Ren lay awake, wondering how a building could be abandoned and inhabited at the same time. Sure, she understood why it might be helpful for a building to *look* abandoned. You could avoid drawing attention to your huge heap of ancient artifacts, for example. You could study things that Jinn had gently described as "outside of university interests."

But wouldn't you want to fix things up a bit? This place had rats scurrying around under the floorboards. Actual *R-A-T-S* rats.

Weak light filtered in the window to her little room, along with ominous sounds: screams and bangs. A siren wailed by on the street below, its flashing light painting Ren's wall red-blue-red-blue. It receded into the distance, leaving her nerves vibrating like a strummed guitar. "This building is protected," Jinn had said without much conviction. "But let me know if it isn't."

Ren shivered in the warm night and pulled her thin sheet in tight. It wasn't the sirens that had her so spooked, or even the spirits. It was their cause. Two words formed in her head, clear and horrible: *Death Walker*. She was sure there was one here. She'd seen the way they plagued cities: scorpions in New York, blood rain in London, and now voices in Cairo.

The Death Walkers were beings evil enough that they knew they would fail the weighing of the heart ceremony — a test to get into the afterlife — and powerful enough to do something about it. They had clung to the edge of the after-life, in between life and death, waiting for an opportunity to escape. An opportunity Alex's mom had given them.

Now they were free and they were getting more powerful. How could this little group of friends hiding in a run-down house stop something so strong? Ren glanced over at the ibis amulet on her night table. Todtman and Alex were confident with their amulets. She was not.

The pale stone ibis shone softly, the image of an elegant, long-necked bird. She took it off to sleep, because she didn't want it in her head when she dreamed. She wondered what would happen if she took hold of it now. The first time she'd used it, it had given her clear images, clear answers. But since then, it seemed to get harder to use the more she tried.

She'd just have to try harder.

Back in school, they'd called her Plus Ten Ren for the sheer volume of extra credit she plowed through. She wasn't going to give up here. Ren threw her sheet to the side, took a deep breath, and reached over and plucked the ibis from the nightstand. She formed a question in her mind: *What are we dealing with?* Then rephrased on the fly: *What are we up against?* As soon as her hand closed around the ancient amulet and the electric energy began coursing through her veins, images flooded her mind.

An old warehouse, dark and empty; the sort of generic disposable cell phone Todtman had given each of them; a swirl of wind-whipped sand on a rocky desert landscape . . . The rapid-fire barrage knocked all words, and all sense, straight out of her head. She let go with a gasp, the amulet thunking down on the nightstand. *What had she seen? What did it mean?*

She looked at the little ibis, glowing softly in the dim light. She wanted to leave it there but forced herself to reach for it once more. "Try harder," she whispered. She formed a new plan. She'd try moving some small object, or maybe opening the door — things the others could do easily with their amulets. But as soon as she grasped the ibis, another barrage of images stopped her cold: the swirl of wind-whipped sand again; a steep, rocky slope; the blazing sun. She felt like the amulet was shouting at her in a language she didn't understand.

What did any of those things have to do with Cairo?

She felt like a failure, and she hated that. She got the same sick feeling she did when she couldn't understand some key concept in class, when she was too confused to move on but too embarrassed to ask the teacher to repeat it.

She'd felt that way with negative numbers. They just hadn't seemed fair to her: How can a number be negative? And she had nearly failed that test. Her father — her brilliant father — had tried to hide his disappointment when he found out, but she'd cried anyway. Now she felt a fresh tear forming in the corner of her eye and wiped it away quickly.

She dropped the ibis back on the table and flopped over in bed, turning her back on the thing. *Forget magic amulets*, she told herself. The test it was giving her wasn't one she wanted to take — not now and honestly not ever. What she needed was a sleeping pill. They had a big day tomorrow. They were going to the Egyptian Museum to meet with Todtman's Supreme Council contact. It had been the first museum to shut down once the Walkers had risen and the mummies had started moving. Todtman had said the man had information about the Lost Spells, and his hushed and hopeful tone had hinted at even more. Those were the kinds of things you needed energy for. She forced her eyes shut.

And that's when she heard a scratching at the door.

Her eyes snapped back open. She waited, listened. There it was again: two more scratches — small, sharp claws on old wood — and then the telltale head bump.

Ren threw back the threadbare sheet and got up. The wood felt oily and half-rotten under her bare feet.

She reached the door, paused for just a second, and then slowly cracked it open. The creature slipped inside, a strand of its ragged linen wrappings catching momentarily on the door frame. Ren's breath caught just slightly — it was a sight she might never fully get used to.

And then . . . The last place she'd seen this mummified cat was 3,500 miles away. Ren had covered the distance by plane — but how had the cat done it? It definitely wasn't on those bony little paws.

"Mmrack," it said softly.

"Hi, Pai," said Ren.

She wasn't ready to let most of the magic and mystery she encountered into her carefully ordered world, but this strange cat she was happy to let in.

There were rats here, after all.

To the Museum

Alex was quickly learning that the first step in hunting down a Death Walker or lost Egyptian antiquities was a stop at the closest museum. They skirted the edge of Tahrir Square and then hustled across the courtyard. It wasn't safe to be out in the open for long, even so early in the morning. This was The Order's home turf.

Still, Alex stared in wonder. Palm trees swayed overhead and the mighty Egyptian Museum loomed before them.

His mom had told him stories of this place the way other moms told stories of Winnie the Pooh, but its massive red-brick walls looked even more striking than he'd imagined. Large marble plaques along the front listed the dynasties of ancient Egypt. And inside, he knew, was an unmatched collection of the art and artifacts of that lost world.

"Yes, it's beautiful," said Todtman, clacking up behind him. "Now hurry!"

As they started up the steps to the grand archway at the entrance, the massive front door swung open like a bank vault. A stocky man in a rumpled suit appeared inside. "Quickly," he said.

Alex looked behind him, checking to see if they were being followed. But then he realized that this man's body language — blocking the door as if trying to keep a dog inside — indicated that he was less concerned about what might get into the museum than what might slip out.

The little group left the bright light and rising heat of Egypt's present and was ushered into the cool, shadowy realm of Egypt's past.

"I am Mr. Hesaan, and on behalf of the Supreme Council of Antiquities I welcome you!" said the man, stepping forward to shake Todtman's hand. "Especially you, my old friend."

But the welcome was cut short as the big door swung shut and a chorus of dry, skittering whispers rose up and faded like a swirl of dead leaves.

"Yes," said the man, diligently turning a series of large locks with a ring of keys. "This place is haunted now. Quite haunted. The whole city is, but especially" — he clicked the last lock shut and turned back toward the massive hall — "this place."

Alex's eyes had adjusted to the dim light now, but the shadows remained deep, the silence charged, and the air heavy.

"Are we alone?" said Todtman.

Hesaan frowned. "We are never alone, I fear," he said. "But there are no other people here. The other entrances are boarded shut, and that is the first time I've opened the main door today."

Alex understood the rumpled suit now. "You slept here?"

"The treasures of Egypt must be protected," said Hesaan with a shrug. "And no one else will stay. I sleep in my office with a cricket bat and swat away the shadows."

Alex saw Ren shudder slightly and took a step closer to her.

"But now you are here!" said Hesaan, clapping Todtman on the back in a way that made him wince. "All of you. And you have more than cricket bats."

"Cricket's like baseball, right?" said Luke.

"Far superior," said Hesaan, but his eyes were on everyone except Luke. "Three amulets in one place. I never thought I'd see this day."

Hesaan's eyes flicked toward the amulets hanging from Todtman's and Ren's necks. Alex wore his under his shirt. The polished stone and copper beetle was chunkier and more conspicuous than the others. Plus, he liked to think of it as a concealed weapon: the only one that could activate the Book of the Dead and banish the Death Walkers.

Hesaan's eyes lingered for just a moment on the spot where the scarab rested under Alex's shirt, then he straightened up and got to business. "So," he said. "What is it you need from the Supreme Council?"

He was addressing Todtman, but the doctor had turned to look back at the front door for some reason. It unnerved Alex. The falcon amulet was known as the Watcher for a reason. If Todtman wasn't ready to answer, though, Alex was.

"We are looking for the Lost Spells!" he said. But at exactly the same moment, Ren said: "We need the Book of the Dead."

"You seem to need a great many things," said Hesaan.

"Perhaps I can clarify," said Todtman. Everyone listened carefully as the man who had led them this far laid out their next steps.

"We have already found and sent back two Death Walkers. There is another one in Cairo, that much seems clear, and to battle it, we would need the Book of the Dead." He nodded toward Ren, who couldn't resist giving a triumphant little nod in return.

But faster than Alex could say "teacher's pet," Todtman continued: "But I believe that without the Lost Spells — the spells that started all of this — we can only send the Walkers back to where they were before, clinging to the edge of the afterlife . . . waiting for another door to open . . ."

Alex risked a quick glance at Ren, who now looked slightly betrayed.

"You think they could come back," said Hesaan.

The thought was like an icicle down Alex's back.

"Yes," said Todtman. "If our enemies get to the Lost Spells first, the Walkers will be beyond harm. The Order will be unstoppable."

"I see," said Hesaan as he began walking again, leading the little group deeper into the large, shadowy room.

"You said you might have some information?" asked Todtman.

"Yes," Hesaan said, taking a look around to confirm that they were alone. "Dr. Bauer is here, in Egypt. Or at least she was."

"Wait, what, where?" Alex blurted. His mother *was* here!

Hesaan looked at him, something like pity in his expression, and answered, "Her passport was scanned in Luxor, ten days ago. In the little airport there."

"And then?" demanded Alex.

"And then nothing," said Hesaan. "It is a much smaller city than Cairo — half empty these days with the trouble in the country — and the council has many people there, but there has been no further sign of her."

"Why was she in Luxor?" said Todtman.

"I have a guess," said Hesaan. "I believe she first found the Lost Spells near Luxor — in the Valley of the Kings." Hesaan gestured down at a large table in front of him.

It was covered by a large, intricately detailed replica of a desert landscape, the hillsides and valleys cut away in places to reveal side views of underground chambers. Tombs. As Alex scanned the model, he recognized famous landmarks: the tomb chapel of Hatshepsut, cutaway views of the largest and most ornate tombs, and then one of the smallest but most important. The tomb of King Tutankhamun.

"Maggie got the Lost Spells from the Valley of the Kings?" said Todtman.

"I can't say for sure," admitted Hesaan. "But when she first brought them in, she arrived on an overnight train from the valley. She would not say exactly where she found the Spells when I asked. The spot had kept them safely hidden for thousands of years. She was protecting it."

Todtman sized up Hesaan carefully. "You think she's gone back to Luxor to return the Spells to their hiding place."

Hesaan looked over at him. "Why else would she come back?"

A sudden, sharp noise echoed through the room. It was no phantom whisper this time. The big front door was swinging open!

Hesaan looked down at the keys he'd used to lock it, still in his hand.

Morning sun spilled into the murky gray of the museum. For a brief moment it clearly outlined a single figure: very thin, the skull of a lioness on her head.

"Peshwar," Todtman whispered.

Then other figures rose up to join her.

A Red-Hot Sledgehammer

"The Supreme Council forbids your entrance!" shouted Hesaan, a brave man even without his cricket bat.

"Government entities mean nothing to us," said Peshwar, her voice a hoarse, harsh scratch. "We are the law now."

How had The Order known they were at the museum? The friends had taken every precaution to avoid being followed, but once again, here they were. And this time, Peshwar had waited until the Keepers were inside — until they were trapped.

As she walked through the door, Alex realized that it wasn't a mask she was wearing. It was the actual skull of what must have been a massive lioness. She gazed out through the eye sockets in the sun-bleached bone. Her suit from the day before had been replaced by thick, blood-red robes.

Hesaan maintained his defiant pose, standing tall in the center of the room. But his next words were softer, just loud enough for those around him to hear: "We must run."

A lean, stone-faced man came through the door after Peshwar, and a second was on the threshold.

Alex's left hand was already on his amulet. He felt the copper wings of the ancient beetle dig into the soft flesh of his palm as his pulse began to race. His mind cleared, and one thought formed very clearly:

We did enough running yesterday.

His right hand shot up, his fingers spread slightly. The scarab was a symbol of resurrection in ancient Egypt, and his amulet dealt with life, death, and rebirth. But those things took many forms in this thirsty land. *The wind that comes before the rain . . .* As the words formed in his mind, a column of desert air rose up and rushed forward. In front of him, glass display cases shivered and stone statuary wobbled. Alex bunched his fingers more tightly, and the wind gained focus and strength.

The lioness staggered backward a few steps, her robes whipping in the sudden gust. The Order thug steadied her and the two leaned forward into it, like sailors weathering a storm on deck. If either of them had been the target, the attack would have been a failure. But Alex had another goal in mind.

The heavy main door slammed shut. A thick crunch and a pitiable wail could just be heard over the whipping wind as the forearm of the man about to enter was pinned in place by the heavy door, with the rest of him still stuck outside.

"That's gonna leave a mark," said Luke, wincing.

Alex refocused just in time to see a red glow sprout from Peshwar's closed right hand and form itself into something like an icicle: a jagged, uneven shard of crimson light. No

35

sooner had Alex spotted it than she had whipped her hand back behind her head.

"Watch out!" said Todtman.

Peshwar's hand came forward in a blur, and the glowing energy dagger flew through the air — straight toward Ren. Alex looked over and saw her squinting at the glowing missile, trying to understand rather than avoid. He leapt toward her and gave her a two-handed shove. As she stumbled backward out of the way, the blood-red slice of light pierced the elbow of Alex's outstretched left arm. He felt a staggering jolt of pain, as if someone had hit his funny bone with a red-hot sledgehammer.

"Aaaaaah!" he shouted, dropping to one knee.

"Alex!" called Ren, from the spot where she'd fallen.

He looked up and saw her scrambling to her feet, the image refracted by the tears welling up in his eyes. Another blade of crimson light sizzled through the air as Ren headed toward him. She dodgeballed it with a quick stop and start, and it missed her stomach by inches. He could feel its heat as it passed between them — and hear the crunch of its impact.

"No!" cried Hesaan.

Alex whipped his head around in time to see a large alabaster urn topple off its pedestal. It hit the marble floor and shattered. Ancient ash spilled out and was instantly pulled up in a swirling dust devil. As the gray particles rose, the whispers rose up with them, louder now, angrier. The ash formed a face, deep black eyes and an open mouth, and then dispersed, falling back to the floor. The whispers persisted for a few moments more.

"We cannot fight in here!" called Hesaan, his tone now pleading and desperate.

The lioness disagreed. She had paused only briefly at the sight of the whirling visage, and now her hand glowed red as another energy dagger took form. Behind her, the first Order thug freed the arm of the second, and three more armed men surged through the open door.

"We have to go!" called Ren.

Alex wanted to stay and keep fighting, but he knew Ren was better at calculating the odds than he was. The friends were outnumbered and outgunned this time.

"This way!" called Hesaan.

Ren helped Alex to his feet, tugging him by his good arm. "Does it hurt?" she huffed through the effort.

"Not too bad," he answered, but his arm was hanging limp and a fire burned inside it.

Wall Crawlers

They used a statue and a sarcophagus for cover as they ran. Luke went wide, using his speed and agility to draw some attention from the main group. Alex heard the thick whisper of a silencer — *Ffummp!* — and then a bullet plinked off the heavy stone of the old sarcophagus. The friends made it around the corner and Hesaan squashed his palm into a fat red button on the wall. An alarm began a low, slow wail.

"The police should be here," huffed Hesaan, "sometime today."

"If The Order hasn't paid them not to be," Todtman puffed.

Hesaan slammed a door behind them and quickly locked it.

"At least it will take them some time to break through," he said.

"I doubt it," said Alex. He knew Peshwar's mask could wrangle locks as easily as his amulet, and the door was already opening as they hustled onward.

"Where are we going?" called Ren.

"I know a way," said Todtman, over the sound of his cane's feverish click-clacks. He turned to Hesaan. "Is the old passage still open?"

"How do you know about that?" he said.

"You forget," said Todtman. "I did my college internship here."

Alex looked at Ren, wide eyed: *Todtman in college?*

"This building really *is* old!" said Luke.

They turned the next corner to the sound of rapid footsteps close behind them. Hesaan immediately disappeared into an office while Todtman ran more or less headfirst into a blank stretch of wall.

"Wrong panel," he said with a pained grunt.

He took a quick step to the side and knocked.

Hesaan came barreling back out of the office, a cricket bat held over his head and a maniacal look on his face.

"I'll hold them off!" he yelled as he charged back around the corner.

Alex wasn't sure if Hesaan was buying time for the group or trying to protect the artifacts. A little of both, Alex figured. But then he heard the sharp sound of a pistol handle to the skull and the dull thump of Hesaan's stocky body hitting the floor.

Todtman took a last, longing look toward the spot where his old friend had turned the corner, but his expression quickly hardened. "In here!" he said, pushing a wall panel inward.

It was a secret door, revealing a dark passage beyond. Todtman held the panel open as they all squeezed inside. Alex went through first, then blindly shuffled forward to make room for the others. Once Todtman was inside, the panel snapped shut and light filled the narrow passage, pouring from the eyes of his falcon amulet.

The passage was so narrow that only Ren could walk facing straight ahead. The others had to angle their shoulders to fit.

"Forward, then right," whispered Todtman.

They stepped quietly and tried to calm their labored breathing. Alex held his injured elbow in close — it stung sharply every time he bumped the wall. His body cast a long shadow in front of him, the musty smell of old wood filled his nostrils, and little whirls of dust kicked up, daring him to sneeze. Outside the wall, he heard muffled voices and the crash of objects being overturned. *They're looking for us.* But as they continued on, the noises faded behind them.

"The exit's just ahead," said Todtman in a whisper.

Alex had to give a pretty good push once he reached the end of the passage — bouncing hard against the wall with his good arm — but the old walls finally let them go. They emerged into the side courtyard of the museum, and the heat pounced on them like a waiting animal.

"And that, right there, is why I don't like museums," said Luke, blinking back the bright sunlight.

"I hope Hesaan is okay," said Ren.

"I can't believe he did that," said Alex. But while Ren sounded sympathetic and concerned, Alex was furious. He couldn't help it. He had so many questions for Hesaan — burning questions about his mom, about airports and passports and the Valley of the Kings. And now he might never get to ask them.

"Foreigners!" cried a man, pointing wildly at the group as it crossed the courtyard. "The invasion has begun!"

No one bothered to ask what sort of invasion would begin with two twelve-year-olds, one thirteen-year-old, and an old man. Instead, Todtman quickly hailed a taxi and they poured themselves inside as the man continued to rant at their windows, amplifying the angry whispers in his head with his own hoarse cries.

The ride back to the hideout was slow, but Alex didn't mind some time off his feet not dodging energy daggers. A splotch of red around his elbow made it look like he'd dipped it in fruit punch. He gingerly tried to bend it. Sore, but it worked.

"How is it?" said Ren, following his eyes.

"Getting better," he said. "It just kind of nicked me."

It scared him to think what a direct hit would feel like.

They got out of the cab in front of a nicer building a few doors down from the hideout and waited until the driver pulled away before walking down the block.

"How did it go?" Jinn asked as he let them in.

Their body language gave him his answer: Alex holding

his arm, Todtman's limp worse than ever, Luke sweaty and spent, and Ren collapsing into the nearest chair.

"Another ambush," said Todtman.

"Were you followed there?" said Jinn.

Todtman shook his head. "We were careful — and still they were ready. Their timing was perfect . . ." He paused before delivering his verdict: "I believe we have been betrayed."

Splitting Up

Ren sank deeper into the chair as the friends waited for Todtman to finish a hushed phone conversation in the next room. She was more wired than tired, but the old recliner was so worn out that the seat drooped in the middle. And the chair wasn't the only thing giving her a sinking feeling. Todtman's voice was playing on a loop in her head: *We have been betrayed.*

Todtman's phone rang as soon as he returned. He didn't leave the room to talk this time. He didn't even answer, just looked down at the screen and silenced the ring.

"Are you going to get it?" said Ren, though what she really meant was: *Why aren't you going to get it?*

"It is Hesaan," he said.

Jinn looked over. He clearly knew the name.

"Don't you want to see if he's okay?" said Ren.

"He is well enough to make a call," said Todtman.

"Talk to him! He could be really hurt," she exclaimed — and then, embarrassed, realized what the others had already figured out.

Ren had a habit of trusting highly educated people, but now she saw it. The first Order ambush had been outside the apartment the Supreme Council had arranged, and the second was at the museum it ran. And Hesaan was their contact at the Supreme Council. "Hesaan . . ."

Todtman nodded.

He waited for the call to end and then checked the voice message. It lasted about ten seconds. Ren heard a faint but rapid-fire barrage of words and saw Todtman's frown sink lower.

"What did he say?" said Alex.

"He says that his head hurts . . . and they are gone."

"That dude's lucky to still be making calls," said Luke.

"He says he was knocked out cleanly as soon as he turned the corner," said Todtman. "Otherwise he's sure they would have killed him. He says."

But it was clear from Todtman's tone that he wasn't sure of that at all.

"So he's a traitor," said Luke, more as a statement than a question.

Todtman looked at him carefully. "Possibly."

"I hate it when people switch teams," Luke said.

Jinn must have been thinking the same thing. He turned to Todtman. "Hesaan has been here," he said, the concern clear in his voice. "Many times."

A jolt of panic shot through Ren. *What if their safe house wasn't so safe?*

"We need to get out of here," Alex blurted, his voice loud, his words rushed. "We need to get to the Valley of the Kings! You heard what Hesaan said about the Spells, about my mom. She could be there right now."

He was impatient and ready to go, as usual — but Ren felt an instinctive need to check him. His obsessive determination to find his mom had nearly gotten them killed in London. "Yeah, but, Alex, we can't trust Hesaan!"

Alex gaped at her, a stung expression on his face. "Yeah . . . but even if he is working for The Order, he thought we were about to get captured when he told us that. Captured or worse." He flapped his injured elbow. "Why would he lie?"

"Why would he tell the truth?" she countered.

"Children!" said Todtman, a word that made Ren grind her teeth. "We do not know if Hesaan betrayed us, but he *was* telling the truth about Dr. Bauer's passport. The call I made was to the Transportation Authority . . ."

"You have a contact there, too?" said Ren.

"Not exactly," said Todtman. "In Egypt, right now, you see —"

"He means he bribed someone," said Jinn, sparing them all a speech on the causes and consequences of corruption.

"So my mom really did come back here," said Alex, wearing an expression like someone had slapped him. "After she disappeared from New York . . ."

His voice trailed off, and for a moment all the unspoken truths hung in the air. The fact that Alex's mom and the

Lost Spells had disappeared from the Met at the same time had made sense when they thought The Order had taken them both. But now that they knew The Order didn't have either, and that his mom was on her own, it meant she had to have them. It meant she was on the run — without her son.

Ren watched him wrestle with this reality and felt bad. She sympathized with his blind belief in his mom — but did she share it? She liked Dr. Bauer, and knew she'd sacrificed everything to save Alex. But she'd also made a mess of things in the process.

"But ten days is a lot of time," said Todtman. "I just wish there was some way to be sure this is still the right path." He turned toward Ren.

"What?" she said cautiously.

"Perhaps you could use the ibis . . ."

Now all eyes shifted to her. She squirmed in her seat. *Nuh-uh*, she thought. The idea of fielding another baffling barrage of images in front of everyone and then admitting that she didn't know what it meant caused her pulse to rise, her stomach to sink, and pinpricks of sweat to break out on her forehead. And it didn't help that Todtman and Alex were so good with their amulets. *No thank you very much.* She needed to find some way to say no without seeming worthless, and then she realized . . . "I already used it."

"When?" said Todtman, surprised.

"Last night," she said. "I picked it up and . . ."

"Yeah?" said Alex eagerly. Even Jinn and Luke were leaning forward now.

She considered her next words carefully: "And I saw something."

That's true, she thought. She'd definitely seen *something* . . .

"What was it?" said Todtman, his eyes drilling into hers.

She looked around one more time. She wanted them to stop staring at her. She wanted her amulet to help out, like the others did. And more than anything, she didn't want to look dumb.

"I saw the Valley of the Kings," she heard herself say.

For a second she panicked. Had she really? She pictured it again. The swirling sand devil on hard ground, the rocky slope, the blazing sun . . . *Definitely the desert*, she told herself. *And it did seem more like a valley than open desert, where there would be deep, shifting sand dunes* . . .

Alex pumped his fist, their earlier argument instantly forgotten. "You are getting better with that thing, Ren-bo!" he said.

"You are an ibis baller," said Luke.

Even Todtman said, "Impressive."

Ren felt herself blushing. *Was she sure?*

They were all so impressed, all so happy with her . . . *She was sure enough*.

"Thanks," she said. "I've been practicing."

"It is time for you to leave Cairo," Todtman said.

Ren parsed the pronouns. "You're not coming with us?"

Todtman shook his head. "I will stay here for now. This leg is no match for deserts and valleys, and there is still much to be done in this city. I need to find out what The Order is planning, and what sort of evil is plaguing this city."

"And, uh, what exactly are we looking for?" said Luke, never afraid to ask a question twice.

"For my mom," said Alex.

Todtman nodded. "And the Lost Spells."

So they had their mission, and Ren had no doubt it would be a dangerous one. They were splitting up and heading to the blazing desert without their leader — and to the city of ancient tombs beneath.

"I cannot overstate the importance of this," said Todtman. "The Spells may be powerful enough to end this all, to set things right. But if The Order finds them first, they will be unstoppable." He paused. His English was excellent, but it was not his first language. He searched for the phrase that would make his meaning clear. And then he found it. "From now on," he said, "it is winner take all."

Highly Trained

Luke took a long sip of bottled water, wiped his mouth, and said, "Did we just get our butts kicked back there or what?"

The three of them were sitting around a small fold-down table in the dining car of the overnight train to Luxor. Empty soda cans, snack wrappers, and crumpled napkins jittered lightly on the tabletop. Alex and Ren were on one side of the table and Luke was on the other. Their backpacks were piled in the empty spot. The last thing they wanted was company.

"Kind of," admitted Alex. He felt embarrassed about it, like it was his fault they'd been chased across half of Cairo. "And not just our butts." He looked down at his elbow, cradled against his side.

"Oh yeah," said Ren. "How is that?"

He shrugged. He could move it without too much pain now.

"Well at least you can fight back," said Ren. "Thanks for shoving me out of the way, but I wasn't much use."

Alex glanced at the ibis, bouncing slightly over her T-shirt

49

from the motion of the train. "You can't, like, move anything with that?"

"No," said Ren. "Well . . . I think maybe I moved a paper-clip once. But that might have been the wind."

"What's it like?" said Luke, a mix of interest and jealousy in his voice, as if he were asking about playing some hot new video game.

"Awesome," said Alex at the same moment Ren said, "Awful."

The boys looked at Ren: Bad news is always more interesting. She turned to look out the window, avoiding their eyes. "I guess it's not so bad," she said. "But sometimes it's like . . . having a computer virus in my head. Like it's just in there showing me stuff and, I don't know, I guess I just don't like it having access to my hardware, you know?"

Alex didn't. He'd spent twelve years sick and weak, barely able to throw a ball. Now he could lift a refrigerator with his amulet, and he wouldn't give it up for anything. But he knew Ren. He'd seen her notebooks full of lists and knew how much she needed everything to make sense. "Well, at least it let us know about the Valley of the Kings."

"We already knew about that," said Ren.

"Yeah, but you, like, confirmed it," said Alex.

"I guess," said Ren, turning back to the window.

Alex didn't know why she was avoiding his eyes, but he let her. He felt pretty good about where they were, and grateful to his friend for helping to get them there. He looked out the window, too, as the train rumbled southward toward the best lead they'd had since his mom had disappeared. A clear mission plus forward motion made him feel like a bloodhound, hot on the trail. He knew his mom better than anyone. Maybe he could spot signs of her — maybe she was even leaving them for him. He indulged in these idle fantasies until Luke interrupted.

"What are we gonna do once we get out there, anyway?"

Alex answered immediately. "We can use the amulets. Mine can detect the undead, and I think it can detect the magic that makes them. I can always kind of tell when there's a Book of the Dead around, so the Lost Spells should really light it up."

As he said it, it occurred to him that maybe that was how his mom had found the Spells in the first place, back when she had the amulet. He paused before turning back to Ren and adding: "And you can get more info from the ibis, too."

Ren didn't answer, just shrugged and turned back to the window. For a while, they all watched the Nile River roll by. Alex pictured the big map of Egypt in his mom's office at the Met, the Nile running the length of it like a crooked spine. They were heading more or less due south along the river, toward the Valley of the Kings. He'd seen pictures of it. The valley itself wasn't much more than a sunbaked, sand-swept bowl. But carved into the hard, dry ground underneath it was a city of the dead unmatched on earth. That's where his mom had been . . . *Was she still there?*

"I'll tell you one thing," said Luke after a while.

"Yeah?" said Alex.

"I'm glad to be out of that city. People were crazy."

"Yeah, things are supposed to be a little quieter outside Cairo," said Alex. "According to the news and stuff."

"Not where we're going," added Ren. "I read there's a lot of looting."

Alex nodded. He'd read about people robbing the ancient tombs and temples, too, taking advantage of the chaos in the country. He took a sip of his soda and Luke took a big gulp from a jumbo-sized bottled water. Ren popped a potato chip into her mouth.

For a while, anyway, they were just three young Americans on an overnight train trip. With the betrayals of Cairo behind them and their deepest doubts pushed to the corners of their mind for the moment, they could almost think of it as an adventure. They all saw the businessman across the aisle, of course — his large frame and expensive suit made him hard to miss.

They just didn't realize he was watching them, too.

An hour later, it was time for bed. None of the friends had slept well in Cairo, and the rumbling train didn't seem too promising in that regard, either.

The door to the sleeper car felt thin and flimsy as Alex

slid it closed. He clicked the little plastic handle of the lock. It seemed more like a toy lock than a real one. "Think I should try to tie this shut — or put something in front of it, maybe?" he said to Luke. It was just the two of them. Ren was bunked with an elegantly dressed Egyptian woman in a separate sleeper car.

Luke looked over at the flimsy door and shrugged. "Think we're cool," he said.

Alex let it go. He didn't want to seem paranoid.

Luke went back to searching through his pack for his brand-new toothbrush. Todtman had given them a thick roll of Egyptian bills, and they'd peeled off a few layers to replace their lost luggage at a department store near the train station.

"Think I saw a smile from you back in the dining car," said Luke. "Just for a second."

Alex managed another sheepish smile. "Yeah, maybe. Sorry if I've been really gloomy and stuff."

"No problem, cuz. I know you got a lot on your weird little mind."

It seemed like an invitation to talk, and Alex took it. He really had been keeping a lot to himself. "It's just, I don't know, I feel like we might finally be on the right track."

"That's cool," said Luke. "Know something I don't?"

"Well, I know my mom has been to the Valley of the Kings before, like a bunch of times," he said. "Not sure if I mentioned that."

"Oh yeah?" said Luke, finally locating the toothbrush and straightening up. "When was that?"

"Just, you know, before all this . . ."

Luke began brushing his teeth. With the door closed, it felt like a sleepover. His cousin had been way too cool for him back in New York, too obsessed with sports to pay attention to his sick, nerdy cousin. But out here, it felt like they were on the same team.

Luke spat foam into the sink, splashed water on his face, and called top bunk. Alex looked at the cramped bottom bunk and groaned. Then he took his turn at the room's tiny sink. It looked like the sink in an airplane lavatory, only smaller, dingier, and with a sign that read: DO NOT DRINK THE WATER; A CUP OF POTABLE WATER HAS BEEN PROVIDED.

Alex looked around and saw two clear plastic cups: one empty and the other full and covered with shiny silver foil. Alex picked up the full one and saw a small swirl of sediment kick up from the bottom.

"Dude, did you already drink your water?" he said to the top bunk.

"Proper hydration is important," came the reply.

"This water doesn't even look all that clean."

"You should see the stuff that comes out of the faucet."

Alex peeled back the foil and sniffed. Smelled okay.

He brushed his teeth with the water from the cup, clicked off the light, and dropped into the bottom bunk.

"You awake?" Alex said to the bed above him. He thought maybe they could talk some more, but there was no response. Now that Alex had gotten used to the rhythmic rumble of the train, he could make out the sound of deep, steady breathing above him. Luke was already out. Just as well. They planned to get up at sunrise and exit the train before it arrived at Luxor station. If Hesaan had told The Order they were coming, they'd be waiting there.

Alex shifted around and tried to get comfortable on the thin mattress. The train took a corner, decreasing its speed but increasing its bumpiness. Little flashes from passing lights slipped in through the ill-fitting blinds.

Lying awake, he wondered how Ren was doing down the hall. Was she safe there on her own?

Then, inevitably, his thoughts shifted to his mom. Before, he'd been excited — eager as a bloodhound. But with the darkness came the doubts. A bloodhound shouldn't have to chase his master — much less his mother. Why wasn't *she* searching for *him*? He couldn't come up with a theory that made sense. If she was trying to keep him safe, well, that *definitely* wasn't working out. Still, he was mesmerized by the possibility that this train might be headed toward her right now. *But were they? Did she even have the Spells?*

He felt his thoughts getting murkier and tried to concentrate harder, to bring them back into focus. Yes, his mom and the Lost Spells had disappeared on the same day, but she was the one who brought them to New York in the first place.

Why go to all that trouble and then steal them? He knew her better than the others — how devoted she was, and how kind. It didn't make sense to him. *If she had the one thing everyone was looking for — the thing that had started this all and might be able to end it — why would they be hiding her from . . . No, wait . . .* Alex was stumbling over his thoughts. His mind felt gummed up and fuzzy. *Why would she be hiding them from . . . who?*

Something was wrong.

"Luke?" Alex croaked, but he could barely form the word.

Wait, he thought. *Was Luke even in here?* He was having a hard time remembering anything before . . .

Chalky sediment kicking up inside a clear plastic cup . . . Luke's cup empty . . . Luke out cold.

The water. They'd been drugged!

Alex tried to get up but his body felt so heavy that the best he could do was roll out of his bunk. He thunked heavily down onto the floor, his numb body barely registering the impact. His breathing suddenly felt as thick and labored as his thoughts. He managed to raise his right hand up and flop it limply against the wall until he hit the light switch.

The room brightened, but his vision blurred.

"Luuuuke!" he wailed, but it came out as little more than a breathy whisper.

He paused to gather more breath, to try again. And that's when he heard the door's little lock click back. Alex tried to turn his head, but it was taking too long. He flopped over onto his back and looked up as the door slid open.

It was the beefy businessman from the dining car. The man stood there for a moment, his large frame outlined against the black windows behind him, the Egyptian night rushing by. Alex now understood just what sort of business he did, and for whom. The man took a long, quiet step forward and closed the door behind him.

He looked down at Alex, smiled, and shook his head. Then he dropped a small metal key into the right pocket of his suit jacket and took a loop of white plastic out of the left . . . a zip tie. Alex had seen them before, had felt them cutting into the skin of his wrists and hands. Once they were on, they had to be cut off.

Alex flopped his hand around his chest and found his amulet. But it was under his T-shirt, and getting it out from under there seemed impossible. He pushed his hand up to his neck but his fingers were too numb to grab the thin silver chain.

"Luke," Alex said through lips he couldn't quite feel. The soft mumble was mostly drowned out by the rumbling train. But the next sound was much louder . . .

KKLONNK! he heard as a hand shot out from the top bunk and clocked the intruder in the head with a shiny new ten-pound dumbbell.

THWUMMP, he heard as the man collapsed heavily to the floor. His forehead smacked Alex's shin, but Alex barely felt it.

Luke's head appeared over the edge of the bunk.

"I couldn't let him take you," he said. "You'd never come back."

Alex stared at him incredulously. "But . . . you were drugged," he managed. "The water . . ." His words were soft and slurred, but Luke seemed to hear them all right.

Luke raised his eyebrows. "Like I said: *proper* hydration is important. All my coaches say that. And that water did *not* look proper. I poured it out. I've got a big bottle of water anyway."

"Oh yeah," said Alex.

Luke ignored the skinny ladder leading up to his bunk and vaulted down to the floor. He was wearing a T-shirt, shorts, and tube socks, and looked exactly two sneakers short of game-ready. He left the dumbbell behind and brought out the oversized water bottle.

"I think you should take a drink," he said, glancing back to make sure the intruder was still out cold.

Alex fumbled with the bottle and missed his mouth slightly at first, but eventually he got everything lined up and guzzled down at least a pint of lukewarm, possibly Luke-warm, water. His head began to clear a little.

"What should we do with this guy?" said Luke, looking down at the large lump on the floor.

Alex thought about it and then, very slowly, turned his head and looked out the window.

After a few more minutes and another pint of water, he was ready. They waited for the night porter to pass and then

58

dragged the guy out into the hall. The next time the train slowed down to take a turn, it lost more than momentum. They watched the man tumble limp-limbed down a sandy bank and then returned to their car.

Early the next morning, they reached the edge of Luxor.

Ghost Town

They knocked on Ren's door at sunrise, and she slid it
back immediately, fully dressed, bedhead subdued smartly
by a wet comb. "You look awful," she said to Alex. "Not you,
Luke. You just look tall."

"I was drugged," said Alex defensively.

She looked at him dubiously. They'd checked on her the
night before, but hadn't gotten past her startled, angry bunk-
mate. Ren grabbed her pack and left the lady snoring away.
"It's so early," she said once they were all in the hallway. "Do
you really think The Order knows we're coming?"

Alex and Luke exchanged glances. "They know we're
coming," they said together.

Ren didn't ask how they knew, and Alex didn't really have
the heart to freak her out.

The night porter was slumped over, sleeping quietly on a
little fold-down seat at the end of the corridor as they snuck
by. Outside, the blood-orange Egyptian sun was just breaking free from the grip of the horizon.

They stood huddled in the loud, drafty gap between cars, packs on backs and eyes on the little window in the door. Finally, the train began to slow. It reached a road crossing and lurched abruptly to a full stop. Alex could practically hear the collective groan of a hundred passengers bouncing in their bunks. He quickly used his amulet to open the steel door.

On the road outside, the lights flashed and the signals chimed. A handful of early morning motorists stared as three young visitors climbed down, reaching the pavement moments before the train began to chug onward.

The sun crept higher in the sky as they edged toward the center of town, walking slowly and navigating by smartphone. They were heading toward the Luxor docks, where they could catch a ferry across the river to the Valley of the Kings.

"Man, it's already really hot," said Luke, fishing a battered Yankees cap out of his backpack.

"We're in the desert now," said Ren, holding up her latest guidebook.

"Doesn't look like it," said Luke. "Look at all these trees."

Ren lowered the book and raised her eyes. Evenly spaced palm trees lined the road, thick-trunked and branchless, with shocks of fronds on top that offered pools of shade in the sea of sunlight.

"We're on the Nile," explained Alex.

"No, you're in denial," said Luke, and once again Alex couldn't tell if he was joking.

The buildings got closer together as they walked. The whole city of Luxor looked like something out of an Egyptian history book. Alex knew that for thousands of years, this had been Thebes, the capital city and seat of power for some of Egypt's greatest pharaohs. Reminders of their reigns were everywhere. The skyline was low and spiked with temple pylons and minarets. They passed ancient temples and weathered statues. There were legitimately old buildings and new ones designed to look that way.

People stared at them openly as they walked. Cairo had offered overcrowded chaos, but Luxor met them with a sketchy ghost-town vibe. Locals were scarce so early in the morning, making the lean, hungry-eyed men creeping sleepily down the streets seem all the more threatening.

Luke, who looked like an adolescent Viking, got the most stares. Alex got the fewest. Half-Egyptian, thanks to a father he'd never known, and dressed simply in jeans and a T-shirt, he almost blended in. As the sun got higher, the streets remained mostly empty.

"Where is everyone?" said Ren.

"Out of work and scared, I bet," said Alex. "This is a tourist town. With everything that's going on, you'd have to be crazy to visit now."

"Guess that makes us crazy," said Luke. "But it's still a lot nicer than Cairo."

"Should be even quieter once we get out to the Valley of the Kings," said Alex, but even as he formed the words he got the unsettling feeling they might come back to haunt him. Nowhere had been quiet for him lately, not even a sleeper car.

"Yeah, uh, what kind of kings are we talking about?" said Luke as they reached an intersection and waited to cross.

"A lot of the big ones," said Alex. "Ramses, Thutmose, Hatshepsut — though she was technically a queen."

"Really?" said Ren.

"Yeah, a female pharaoh, powerful, too," he said, but they'd lost Luke. Alex glanced over and saw his cousin's eyes fully glazed. "And Tutankhamun," he added. "King Tut."

Luke perked up. "I've heard of him. Dude was really young, right? I mean for a king."

"Yeah, like eighteen when he died," said Alex.

"Why'd he die so young?" said Luke.

Alex shrugged. "A lot of people think he was murdered. His heart was missing when they found him. And my mom says there was a hole in his head."

"Yeah," said Luke, "but people say that about me all the time."

Across the street, Alex found the street sign he was looking for: SHARIA AL-MAHATTA. "I think this will get us to the ferries," he said, "but it will take us past the train station, so we have to be careful."

They needed to get out of town and over to the Valley of the Kings. The train had arrived by now, without them on it. If The Order was waiting for them, they'd probably already figured out the friends had gotten off early — and they'd be searching for them. They walked on, sunlight and open stares bearing down on them; their own eyes alert. They passed Luxor Temple and beyond that, just visible farther up Sharia al-Markaz, Karnak.

The two legendary temple complexes were looming labyrinths of ornately carved stone: thick walls and massive columns, presided over by towering statues of the great pharaohs, some of them thirty feet tall. Alex, a museum kid to the core, normally would have longed to stop — but as Alex's eyes scanned every inch of the dock along the river, it wasn't more sights he was looking for.

How many times had his mom talked about these places: this city, and the valley beyond? And now they *knew* she'd been here, just ten days earlier. Had they just missed her, Alex wondered, or were they about to find her? Maybe she was just beyond them now, in the valley. If she really was hiding, what better place than this forbidding desert that she knew so well? For the one-million-and-first time, he imagined finding her. He would run up and hug her, he knew that, but what would his first words be: *"I missed you,"* or *"Why did you leave me?"*

They climbed aboard the waiting ferry and paid their fares. They quickly headed inside the cabin of the fat-bottomed boat, where it was cooler and they were finally out of open view. The ferry had been built for an army of tourists, but it was nearly empty as it pulled away from shore.

"Which way are we headed?" said Luke. "I'm all turned around."

"West," said Alex. "The dead were always buried on the western bank, because the sun dies there every night."

"Great," said Luke sarcastically. "Dead and buried . . . Let's go there."

As Alex turned to gaze out the window at the swift, dark waters of the Nile, he could feel the copper wings of the scarab hot against his skin. It was the Returner, the symbol of a traveler between the world of the living and the world of the dead. And Alex *had* been in both worlds.

A smile crept onto his face.

"Yes," he said. "Let's."

The Far Shore

"It's so green," said Ren as the ferry bumped slowly into its moorings.

Alex looked around. The western bank was lined with fat-trunked trees and dense bushes, all soaking up the water that had given birth to Egyptian civilization five thousand years earlier, and sustained it ever since.

As they filed off the boat, a few returning passengers filed on. Two of them moved gingerly, as if very old or injured. As they shuffled by, Alex couldn't help but suck a sharp breath in through his teeth.

Their faces and arms were horribly burned. And judging by their stiff, pained movements, that wasn't all.

"Don't stare," a voice whispered.

Alex turned and saw a tall woman with dark brown hair pulled back in a no-nonsense ponytail. His heart nearly stopped. But then he met her gaze, and instead of his mom's steely blue-gray eyes, he saw a soft shade of hazel looking back at him. She looked away, turning to face one of the boat's crew.

"*Shukran,*" she said, taking a tightly wrapped paper bundle from him and discretely slipping him a few folded bills.

"*Al'awf,*" he said, nodding slightly.

"I wasn't staring," said Alex, when she turned back to him.

"You were," she said, not harshly, but firmly enough to settle the matter. She was wearing threadbare khaki pants and a short-sleeved, button-up shirt that may once have been white. On her head was a faded red baseball cap with the white *H* of Harvard on the front. On her feet, the same sort of battered leather boots his mom had always packed for trips to the desert.

Ren eyed the cap. She was the type of twelve-year-old who already had a first-choice college picked out, and Alex knew that was it. "I'm Ren," she said.

"I'm . . ." the lady began before pausing a beat. Alex had seen his mom do that, too, deciding whether to introduce herself as *Dr. Bauer* or *Maggie.* He knew immediately this lady was an academic. "Isadore," she continued, "but you can call me Izzie. All of the other crazies out here do."

"How do you know we're crazy?" said Alex, not bothering to deny it.

Izzie's only answer was another small smile and a quick look behind them for any signs of parents.

"What happened to those people?" asked Ren. "Were they in a fire?"

"Sunburn," said Izzie. A strange expression flashed across her face. "They say it happened last night," she said softly.

"That's impossible," said Alex, remembering the open blisters on their faces, the wet stains oozing out from under the fresh gauze on their arms.

But Izzie was already stepping briskly off the dock, and her only response was an over-the-back wave good-bye.

They waded out into the parking lot, a fresh blast of heat hitting them as soon as they stepped on the sun-softened blacktop. Alex had no idea how two people could get such brutal sunburns at night, but he could easily see how it would happen during the day out here. He glanced at Luke's Yankees cap and wished he'd thought to pack his Mets cap — sickly for most of his life, he'd always identified with underdogs.

Alex looked around. They were at the gateway to what had long been one of the world's top tourist destinations. But they seemed to be the only tourists there today, and a handful of eager taxi drivers were beginning to circle. Rising up in the distance behind them was the first phalanx of hotels.

"A real hotel would be nice," said Ren a little wistfully. "No rats . . ."

"We can't get a hotel," said Alex, lowering his voice as the first of the drivers approached. "Three kids with U.S. passports . . . How long do you think it would take The Order to find out about that?" Left unsaid: *There's no way my mom will be there, either.*

Alex waved off the first few taxi drivers and headed for the edge of the parking lot. The other two followed.

"Well, where, then?" said Ren.

"Yeah," said Luke. "What's your big idea?"

Alex had decided after nearly getting nabbed in the little shoe-box sleeper car: No more tight spaces. He pointed up at the low-slung building in front of them. The sign above it was crowded with a few dozen words in Arabic, but only two in English: CAMPING SUPPLIES!

"We go no farther," the taxi driver said firmly. He pulled over to the side of the road, the desert stretching out around them.

"We're not even in the Valley of the Kings yet," Alex said, scanning some of the signs next to the road.

"Exactly," said the driver. "It is too hot in the valley now."

It was one o'clock on the nose, and the sun was almost directly overhead. But Alex wasn't sure that's what the driver meant by "now." Those burned arms and the bandages . . .

"Has something happened in the Valley of the Kings?" said Alex. "Has something changed?"

"Everything has changed," the driver said bitterly. "I leave you here, along with the other . . ." He paused to find the right phrase and then spat it at them. "Thrill seekers."

They were dumped out into the sizzling heat along with all their stuff: their small backpacks stuffed inside big, new ones. It definitely wasn't much of a thrill. Alex glanced up into the cloudless sky and was blinded by the blazing sun.

"Where now?" said Ren.

This time Alex had no answer. "Do I look like the kind of kid who's been on campouts before?"

"I have," said Luke. "Hiking's awesome for the legs. Throw in some rock climbing, and it's a killer total body workout."

"I'm not looking for a killer workout," said Ren. "Just, you know, not getting killed."

"Nice one, short-stuff," said Luke, pointing at her with both index fingers. "Point is: The first thing you need to do is find shelter. Like from the wind —"

"Or the heat," said Alex, pulling his new hat out of his backpack. It was round and flat on top, with a bill in the front and a curtain of cloth in the back that covered his ears and neck.

Luke and Ren glanced at each other and laughed softly. Alex pretended not to notice as he put it on.

The landscape was mountainous at the edge of the valley. Long ridges scraped the sky in both directions, jagged, rocky fins erupting upward from the sunbaked ground. When Alex thought of desert, he thought of softly drifting sand, but the rim of the valley was stony and hard. He kicked the toe of his new boot into the ground and got a solid thud in return. He could feel the heat radiating up from it right through the leather. A sense of dread descended on him. *This is an unforgiving landscape*, he thought.

He turned and looked toward Ren. Luke did, too.

"What are you guys looking at me for?" she said.

But they weren't looking at her; they were looking at her amulet.

"Ask it where the best shelter is," said Alex.

Ren's reluctance was obvious: She refused to even look down at the ibis.

"Come on," said Luke. "It's hot out here."

He had settled into a role that was less decision-maker than tie-breaker, joining Ren in laughing at Alex one minute and siding with Alex against her the next. Now she was outvoted. She frowned and then . . . "Wait!" she said. "It's telling me something."

"Really?" said Luke, gaping at the amulet.

"You aren't even holding it," said Alex, incredulous. Did she no longer need to do that? Had Ren somehow leap-frogged him in amulet use?

"Yeeessss," said Ren, her voice sounding ghostly and far away.

They both watched, rapt, as she quickly knelt down.

"The power of the ancient amulet is telling me . . ."

Her hands moved quickly, and a moment later she stood back up.

"To use my eyes."

She was holding the new binoculars they'd just purchased at 40 percent off.

"There's some shadow up there, along the top of the

ridge," she said. "Looks like good shelter. And wait . . . Yeah . . . There are some people camping up there already."

"I guess those are the 'thrill seekers,'" said Alex. "Is there space for us up there? I mean, without getting too close?"

"Plenty," said Ren.

"Let's go there," said Luke, hoisting his pack onto his back. "We can at least follow people who know what they're doing."

Base Camp

The slope of the ridge was gentler toward the base, and they stayed low until they skirted around the other campsite. Ren knew the deal. They'd been ambushed repeatedly. None of them were in an especially trusting mood — and the phrase "thrill seekers" didn't inspire much confidence, especially the way the taxi driver had said it. They were dripping with sweat by the time they dropped their stuff half a mile later, on a small, reasonably flat plateau just beneath the top of the ridge that encircled the valley.

"How about here for the tent?" said Alex.

"Okay," said Ren. "You two set your tent up over there. I'll set mine up over here."

They all dropped their heavy packs onto the hot ground.

"You bought your own?" said Alex.

"Uh, *yeah*," she said. "You boys stink."

Alex stood there, two half-moons of sweat under the arms of his T-shirt, and said, "Then why have I been lugging this circus tent around all day?"

He tugged an oversized roll of green nylon from his pack as Luke removed the stakes and collapsible poles from his. Ren didn't answer, already kneeling down to remove a small, light-blue pup tent from her pack.

She unfolded the directions and began following them carefully. Fifteen minutes later, she was done. She stood back and considered her work: It looked exactly like the picture on the package. She nodded and looked over at Alex and Luke.

It looked like they were playing Twister with twenty pounds of nylon. The instructions, utterly ignored, had blown halfway down the slope.

"Little help?" said Alex, looking over.

Ren considered it, but it was really hot out in the sun. They would have to settle for encouragement. "Good luck!" she called, and then climbed into her little tent to unpack. "Let me know when you're done!"

She pulled her stuff inside the warm, plastic-smelling air of the tent and spread out her new foam pad. She checked her phone. No surprise: no service out here in the desert. She wished she could lie down and rest, but they had a mission to get to. For just a second, she thought of that. Finding the Spells and putting an end to all this — *going home!*

But there was a problem, too. Their plan involved the amulets. Alex's with its radar for the undead and sixth sense for magic. And hers. She looked down at the ibis. The others thought it provided answers. *"Ask it where the best shelter is . . ."* Like it was freaking Google! In her mind, though, it mostly just provided questions. And yet she knew she'd have to use it again — and soon. She got a sick feeling in her stomach. People called it butterflies, but she knew better. It was acid. It was nerves.

Last time, the amulet had shown her a valley — it had basically told them what they already knew. What would it show her this time? And would she understand?

She crawled back out of her tent and stood up into the sunlight. "Time to see the valley," she called.

The boys' tent had taken shape, and that shape was lop-sided. "Good enough," said Alex, standing up and swiping his hands together.

Luke looked at the ramshackle structure and high-fived him.

Hiking the remaining distance up to the top of the ridge was hard for Ren with stiff new boots and short legs. The slope got steeper toward the top, and they leaned forward, using their hands and almost crawling. The sun was lower now, and the shade deeper as they neared the crest of the ridge. It should have been cooler, but . . .

"It's a million degrees up here," said Luke. "I'm getting microwaved."

Alex was first to the top. As he ducked his head over the jagged crest and looked down into the valley, he made a face like he'd just stuck his head into a juicy garbage can.

"What is it?" said Ren as Alex ducked back behind the shade of the ridge.

"It's *hot*," he said. "Total blast furnace."

Ren thought he was exaggerating, and then she popped her head over for a look. "Wow," she said, pulling back. "You're right. You could cook dinner in that."

She leaned against the steep, rocky ridge crest and slowly extended her hand. As soon as it hit the sunlight on the valley side, it felt like she was sticking it in an oven.

"I guess that's why the taxi driver wouldn't go in," said Luke, conducting a similar experiment with one chicken-winged elbow.

Ren held up the binoculars and leaned forward.

"Be careful," said Alex.

She nodded and scanned the valley floor as quickly as she could. As she fumbled with the knob to adjust the focus, she felt the metal heating up and her hair practically crisping. The sunlight made it feel as if someone were pressing a hot pan down on the top of her head. She stayed there for as long as she could — and then a moment longer. Finally, when it felt like her head was going to burst into flames, she pulled back into the shade and took a deep, gasping breath.

She held the image in her head: the entire valley shimmering in the heat. It was a vast bowl of sunbaked ground, a sea of tan with patches of lighter sand and darker stone. And then there were the tombs: some little more than gaping holes in the ground, some with small structures and gates. At the edge of her vision, she'd seen some sort of large structure, a temple maybe. And everywhere there were signs and steps and places for large groups of people to line up. But there were no lines today. "There is no one down there," she reported.

"No one?" said Alex.

"No one," she confirmed, and they both knew who he meant. His mom might be smarter than most people, but she wasn't any more heat resistant.

"It would still be a great time to look around," said Alex. "If we could."

"We would straight up burst into flames," said Luke, spelling it out.

"Maybe tonight, once the sun is down," said Alex.

Ren gave him a look. Every single time she had been in a tomb at night, she had nearly died. "Let's go tomorrow morning," she said. "Before the sun is really up."

"Yeah," said Luke, breaking another tie. "I'm more of a morning person."

Alex didn't push it. The valley was uninhabitable, at least during the day, and Ren could see that the discovery had thrown him. She looked at her best friend. *So hopeful*, she thought. *He really thought she'd be there.*

They headed back down the ridge, half walking and half sliding, the sun sinking below the horizon by the time they arrived back at their camp. As their eyes adjusted to the sudden darkness, they saw a campfire burning in the other campsite. They set up their own sad little campfire with two cans of Sterno cooking fuel and sat around it on a sandy stretch of ground. Ren sat between the small pink flames and the other camp, shielding them from view.

She looked around at the dark, quiet desert. *Anything could be out here*, she thought. She remembered Peshwar, a blade of red energy in her hand. Ren's breath caught as she noticed a more immediate glow: a pair of ghostly green eyes approaching from the dark desert. Then she realized how low the eyes were to the ground. She hadn't expected to smile that night, but she did now. "We have company," she said, turning to greet their guest.

Pai walked into the weak glow of the canned fuel. She had something in her mouth: jet black and pointy in all directions. She stalked past Luke, who crab-walked a few feet backward in the sand. "How did that creepy cat get here?" he said.

Ren was wondering the same thing, but mostly she was wondering what that was in Pai's mouth. The mummy cat looked up at Ren, a glimmer of pride in her glowing eyes, and then dropped the fat, black scorpion in the sand at her feet. "For me?" said Ren, staring down at the dead arachnid. "You shouldn't have."

The Valley of the Kings

As early as it was, Alex's eyes snapped open at the first chirps of his alarm. It was finally time to head into the Valley of the Kings. His mind was eager, but his body registered its protest as he sat up. He'd barely slept, having been woken up twice during the night by bursts of light so bright they lit the inside of the tent like a camera flash. At first he was worried they were flares, that someone was out searching for them, but by the time he got the flap unzipped and looked out, the desert was dark again. Lying awake afterward, he began to get a very bad feeling about this place.

Now, as he fumbled around in the weak dawn light of the cramped tent, trying to put his socks on, the feeling became a question. The strange happenings in the valley were starting to fit an all-too-familiar pattern. *What was causing the strange light and incredible heat out here?* he wondered. *What . . . or who?*

It suddenly occurred to him how someone could get a sunburn at night . . . A Death Walker. *Now* he was awake.

He pulled on his second sock in one clean movement and used that sock to kick Luke. "Come on, man," he said. "It's not getting any cooler out there."

Luke groaned and pulled his thin, reflective camping blanket in closer. "Seems pretty cool in here," he said.

"I'm putting my boots on," warned Alex. "Don't make me kick you again."

"I will beat you like pancake batter, little man," said Luke, but he was already sitting up.

Alex adjusted his new hat and exited the tent. He waited impatiently for the others. His mom had been here. He was sure of it. Why else would she come to Luxor? Maybe there were signs in the valley, things only he would recognize . . .

Ren emerged from her tent next. *Finally*, he thought.

"Where's your friend?" he said.

"Back on the hunt, I guess," said Ren.

"Tell her to bring a burger next time," said Luke, emerging from the tent. "Not another bug."

The three friends headed down the slope, Alex in the lead and the others trudging silently a few steps back. They reached the place the taxi had refused to go past the day before, and this time they kept going. The sun was a broken red yolk, leaking upward over the horizon, and the rocky slopes above them were still streaked with deep purple shadows as the group of three entered the Valley of the Kings.

They wouldn't be alone for long.

The walls of the valley loomed above them, holding the low sun at bay and casting the landscape into deep shadow. It felt like a secret world. The hard-packed ground had been worn smooth by the boots of a million tour groups, but it was empty and quiet now. A little swirl of sand swept by them like a toy tornado, and they all watched it — Ren especially — until it collapsed in a knee-high shower of sand. Alex reached up and wiped his forehead. The air was already hot. Too hot for this dim morning hour, but still bearable.

"We won't be able to stay here long," he said, looking up at the sun's ominous glow, growing along the ridgeline. They were approaching the open mouth of the first tomb. "Time to get to work. Use your amulet, Ren."

"You first," Ren countered quickly.

Alex shrugged and took hold of the scarab. Immediately, his pulse quickened and his system revved. It was a physical rush not so different from fear, from the charged moment right before the roller-coaster car plunges downward. He closed his eyes for a few steps, trying to open himself up to whatever the scarab had to say.

The others watched closely as Alex searched his mind for the little shimmer at the edge of his senses that would tell him of magic and death. He let the scarab fall from his hands.

"What?" said Ren, who'd seen him do this before. "Nothing?"

He looked at her, his eyes wide with wonder. "It's every-where," he said.

"Oh, great," said Luke.

Alex didn't know quite how to explain it. The shimmer wasn't at the edge of his senses this time. Instead, it covered them like a fog. But it was blurred, indistinct. Looking for the supernatural activity in a valley full of tombs in a haunted country was like trying to find a puff of smoke in a fog bank. But there were other methods.

They'd passed the first tomb and were about to pass another. It was one of the lesser-known tombs, on the out-skirts of the Valley of the Kings. It was barely even marked. "Let's try in here," said Alex.

"Is it something you sensed?" said Ren, a hint of fear in her voice.

Alex pointed to his left ear. "Something I heard."

The three friends stopped walking and listened. Faint pings and clicks and thumps emanated from the open mouth of the little tomb. Alex reached into his backpack and pulled out his flashlight. He didn't know who was making those noises, but anyone already in the valley might have seen his mom.

Ren reluctantly reached into her pack and pulled out her own flashlight. She clicked it on and looked at the strong light approvingly. "At least we have new batteries," she said.

"Awesome," said Luke. "We can throw them at the mummies."

They crept through a gate of thick, white-painted metal

bars, unlocked and wide open, and into the dark mouth of the tomb. Alex heard Ren groan softly, but he had the opposite reaction. He felt distinctly, undeniably comfortable as they headed down into the sacred ground. It was as if this was where he belonged. He shook his head hard to dislodge the thought.

The pings and clacks and thumps got louder with each step they took, echoing through the narrow tunnel. And then, abruptly, they stopped.

"Uh-oh," said Ren, and as soon as she did, a voice called out in response. "Who's there? Who is that?"

Alex reached desperately for his amulet with his free hand. They'd given themselves away with their flashlights and footsteps. But then he placed the voice.

"Izzie?" he said.

The odd academic from the docks appeared in front of them. Alex's flashlight beam cut across her face and lit the white *H* on her baseball cap. "Oh, it's you," she said. "You kids gave us a scare."

"Us?" said Ren.

Izzie turned and said, "It's okay, Bridger."

As she did, the tunnel behind her began to glow. A man appeared, kneeling next to a portable electric lantern and turning it up. The man wore a stained shirt that hung over his massive gut and an old-fashioned fedora hat that looked almost dainty in comparison. Behind him was a large chamber and two more men.

Alex sized them up in the dim light of the lantern: button-down shirts in the desert, wire-frame glasses, good boots, Izzie's Harvard cap and Bridger's Indiana Jones fedora. He knew this type.

"You're archaeologists," he said, the relief clear in his voice.

"How do you know that?" said Bridger, as if Alex had accused them all of something.

Alex suddenly realized that they all had their hands behind their backs. "Um," he said, his relief fading. "Because my mom is, too. Her name is Maggie Bauer. Dr. Maggie Bauer."

Despite the strange situation, Alex felt a wild, electric hope as he said the words. He was sure they'd know the name. Any archaeologist would right now: her name and probably her face. She was the woman who had found the legendary Lost Spells. *Had they seen her?*

But the group's response was anything but electric. A heavy silence filled the tomb. Small movements cast long shadows in the lantern light, and a distinct chill went through the warm, stale air. "You should go," said one of the men.

Ren tried to thaw things out. "I'm Ren," she said cheerily. "Are you camping up along the ridge?"

"Maybe," said Bridger.

"Well, I'm not waiting any longer," said one of the men. "We barely have another hour."

"Me either," said Bridger, moving away from the lantern.

Alex heard a chipping sound: *plik, plik, plik* . . . And then a chopping sound: *thunk, thunk, thunk* . . . Something was happening along the shadowy walls of the chamber. He swung his own flashlight around for a better look.

He couldn't believe it.

Bridger was standing against the wall with a rock hammer in his hand, dislodging a stone relief. The piece was intricately carved, covered in deep-cut hieroglyphic symbols, and thousands of years old.

"What are you doing?" said Alex.

"If I don't do it, someone else will," said Bridger without bothering to pause his plunder.

"That's tomb robbing!" said Ren.

Alex saw her swing her flashlight toward Izzie, an appeal to the clear leader of the group to control her own. But Izzie was doing the same thing!

She didn't even turn around as the light danced across the back of her sweat-stained shirt. "Stop!" shouted Ren.

Now Izzie turned around. "I'm sorry," said Izzie, shielding her eyes from Ren's accusing flashlight. "I guess you're too young to understand. Only the most important tombs are being guarded now. These objects are vulnerable. We are saving them."

"You are stealing them!" said Alex.

The room grew deathly quiet again. Alex suddenly realized that they were outnumbered by four adults with sharp-tipped hammers in their hands. He didn't care. "My mom would never do this!"

"Well, she's not here anymore," said Bridger.

Alex nearly fell over, a single word echoing like cannon fire in his brain. "What —" he stammered. "What do you mean 'anymore'?"

"Nothing," said Izzie before he'd even finished asking. "Shut up, Bridger. You talk too much. And I will not be lectured by children! It is time for you three to go."

Alex was still staring at Bridger.

He still hadn't answered the question.

"But you're not supposed to be like this," Ren said to Izzie, her words heavy with disappointment. "You're from Harvard."

"Formerly from Harvard," said Izzie. "This is my ticket back . . . Now get out of here."

"Hold on a second," said Bridger, and suddenly the beam of his flashlight played across the front of Ren's shirt. "That's a nice necklace . . . An ibis, isn't it?"

Another flashlight beam swung around, framing the amulet.

Alex instinctively stepped in front of his friend, his hand rising to the amulet around his own neck. "Yeah, I've got one, too, guys."

"Yeah, seriously," said Luke, taking a step toward Bridger. "Back off, man."

"That's enough," said Izzie. "We are not thieves."

Alex didn't bother to point out that she was saying that with a rock hammer in her hand and the dust of ancient limestone on her face. He looked away from her in disdain and turned back to Bridger. He said his next words very clearly. "What do you mean 'anymore'?" His hand was still on his amulet, and he knew he could level this big man with a blast of wind or batter him with his own hammer, but a single sound changed the equation.

Klickk!

In the dim lantern light, Alex couldn't even see which one of them had cocked the gun. He recalculated. He wanted to push the issue, to make the man tell him what he'd meant. If it was just him — and his scarab — he would have. But Ren and Luke were there, too. A single shot in this tight space, a single ricochet . . . Still, he needed to know if this man had seen his mom. "I don't think you understand the danger you're in," said Alex, tightening his grip on the scarab.

Bridger laughed as he switched his hammer to his left hand and removed something from under his untucked shirt with his right. Alex didn't need to wait for the click to know it was a second gun. "I don't think you do, either, little boy."

"Oh, for heaven's sake," said Izzie, stepping forward. "Just tell him, Bridger. We don't want to shoot children."

Bridger made no move to put his very large revolver away, but he relented slightly. "Fine," he said. "I saw Bauer coming out of KV 62 . . . eight, nine days ago. Your mother never did have time for the small stuff." He waved his pistol vaguely around the small tomb to make his point.

Alex gobbled up the fresh information greedily, but that didn't mean he was going to let this guy insult his mom. "Yeah, she never stole it, either!"

Bridger smiled wickedly. "No," he said, "not the small stuff . . ."

Alex took a step toward him; Bridger raised his pistol.

"Enough!" said Izzie. "He told you what he saw. Now do your part and stop wasting our valuable time."

Alex looked around: long shadows, drawn guns, unfriendly faces. "Fine," he said. "Let's go."

The three friends backed carefully out of the desecrated chamber.

"Where are we going?" said Ren as they reached the main tunnel.

"KV 62," said Alex. He knew exactly which tomb that was — there wasn't an Egyptologist's son who didn't — and he understood Bridger's jab, too. KV 62 was no one's idea of "small stuff." And with three little words, Alex clued the others in as well. "King Tut's tomb."

Burned

They crossed the sunbaked boneyard. At first Ren complained bitterly about the tomb robbers, digging deep for something hurtful to say and coming up with: "I hope they never get tenure!" But with sand and hot wind blowing in their faces, it was easier not to talk. Alex leaned forward into it, like a dog tugging hard on his leash.

It wasn't hard to find Tut's tomb. KV 62 was the valley's main attraction, and there were signs for it spread around, in various languages. But time was becoming a major issue. Dawn had become early morning. The sun rose higher, and the heat did, too. It was over 100 degrees already, and climbing rapidly.

"Look," said Alex, pointing. "Here it is."

It was a sad scene as they approached. One of the world's major tourist destinations stood exposed: no lines and no tourists. A broken-down cab puttered around the corner and into view as they approached, as if summoned by the prospect of paying customers. As the kids arrived at the tomb, the driver lowered his window and smiled.

"You are just in time!" he said, his accent thick but his English solid. "I was on my way out of the valley. I can take you!" He gave them a price.

"Could you stay here?" said Ren, pointing toward the tomb. "While we go in?"

The man glanced nervously up at the sun and shook his head. "It will be too hot very soon."

"It isn't even eight," said Alex. He couldn't leave without checking out the tomb. His mom had been inside there — maybe she was in there now!

"You don't understand," said the driver. "The heat. It is not normal. It is not . . ." He searched for the English word and then found it: "Natural."

"One hour," said Luke, and then doubled the price the man had quoted.

"Half hour," said the man, and then tripled it.

They shook hands.

The friends hurried past a large sign out front, with Arabic text on top and below that:

TOMB OF

TUT ANKH AMUN

NO: 62

Alex felt a thrill go through him: history and possibility and fear all at once.

And there was something else. Something he'd sensed. Because as hot as the air was, his amulet was hotter. Even through his shirt, he could feel it: hotter and more electric the closer they got. Now he reached up and wrapped his left hand around it. His internal radar screen lit up, and it was no vague shimmer this time.

"What is it?" said Ren.

Alex answered: "Something big."

Is it the Lost Spells, he wondered, *or something more dangerous?*

"Keep an eye out for the guards," said Alex, as he pushed aside an open metal gate.

The others nodded, eyes wide open, flashlights on, as they plunged into the hushed darkness of the tomb. The friends swung the beams from side to side, on edge and on guard. "Hello!" Alex called. No answer.

His heart pounded with each new chamber they entered. But King Tut's tomb was surprisingly small — only four chambers, like a heart — and it soon became clear that they were alone. The disappointment was a bitter pill, but Alex swallowed it and tried to concentrate on the details around them. The walls were light on paintings and hieroglyphic writing. The boy king had been buried in a hurry and in a tomb meant for someone else. His feet had even been chopped off to fit him into the secondhand sarcophagus. Alex had heard all the theories: disease, murder, betrayal . . . They had just entered the third room, the burial chamber, when Alex heard Ren scream.

He swung his flashlight around, grasping for his amulet with his other hand, but she was already apologizing.

"Sorry, sorry," she said, her own flashlight beam resting on a pile of charred cloth and very white bone. "It's bones," she said. "Skeletons."

Alex didn't scream, but he nearly blacked out. Stars filled his eyes. *Mom?*

"I think we found the guards," answered Ren, a slight tremble in her voice.

Alex forced himself to breathe, to focus. The three friends washed the piled remains with their flashlight beams. Scraps of scorched uniform; the remains of a pistol, its melted barrel drooping down like a water faucet; two skulls, two large rib cages. Men. Alex's horror turned to a guilty sort of relief. The bones were bleached pure white, as if by the sun. He remembered the taxi driver's words: *This heat isn't . . . natural.*

The heat, the flashes of light turning night to day, the bleached bones . . . This confirmed what he'd been thinking.

"I think we might be in trouble, guys," he said. "I think there's a Death Walker in the valley."

Ren turned toward Alex, her eyes wide with both fear and realization. "The heat — it's a plague . . ."

"Oh, great," said Luke.

Ren took out her phone and glanced at the time. "We need to hurry up."

A quick check of the fourth chamber — the now empty

treasury — revealed no more bones. His mom wasn't there, either. He looked down at the amulet that had once been hers. There was no Death Walker here now, no mummies . . . And yet the scarab had lit up as strongly as it ever had. It still felt hot and charged against his shirt. Had he been right? Was it sensing the undead — or the death magic of the Spells? He wanted more time to look around. He knew from experience that tombs hid their secrets well. "How about one more look around?" he said.

"The taxi is going to leave, Alex!" said Ren.

"But . . ." he began.

Luke put his hand on Alex's shoulder. His grip was friendly but definitely firm. "If that dude leaves," he said. "We are toast."

Alex exhaled. Thoughts of his mom jostled with memories of the scorched skeletons. "Okay," he said. They'd have to come back.

They rushed out of the tomb, but as they did he saw something that stopped him cold. "That's weird," he said.

It was high up on the wall near the entrance, half in light and half in shadow: a charcoal-black disk with long, thin lines extending down. Each line ended in an ankh, an ancient symbol for life that looked like a cross with a loop on top.

"What is it?" said Ren, her eyes flicking between the image and the exit. The intense heat from outside was already hitting them.

"It's an Aten. A sun disk. Tut abolished that religion," said Alex, as if explaining who George Washington was. "It shouldn't be here."

"We shouldn't be here, either, bro," said Luke.

Alex knew he was right, but this charred graffiti felt important. He craned his neck for a closer look. If he could just tell how it was made . . . or when . . . And that's when they heard the taxi's engine sputter to life. They pushed through the gate and rushed out to the road — just in time to see the taxi speed away. From the backseat, Bridger and the other two men waved gleefully. The back of Izzie's red cap was just visible in the front.

"Those snakes!" said Ren.

Luke took off running after them, but stopped after only a few steps, already sweating. It was at least ten degrees hotter than it had been half an hour earlier, well over 110 now.

"I can't believe we lost our ride because of some symbol painted on the wall," said Ren, giving Alex a side-eye.

Alex stood in the baking, hard-packed sand and watched the taxi turn the corner. "It didn't look painted," he mumbled, distracted. "It looked burned."

Burned, just like the bones had been.

Just like they were about to be.

"Okay, let's go," said Ren, pointing back the way they'd come, a long and winding route.

"No," said Alex, tilting his head up toward the brutal sun,

his concern rising as the temperature did. "If we don't find a shortcut, we won't make it out alive. You've got to use the amulet."

Ren hesitated, and Alex saw her looking around for options. "Couldn't we go back inside?" she said, looking back over her shoulder.

"All day?" said Luke. "With the bones?"

"Ren, come on!" said Alex. "If a Death Walker did that, it could come back, and we'd be trapped, with no Book of the Dead to fight it."

Ren swallowed. "Fine," she said. "I'll try."

Ren closed her left hand around the ibis. Even in the blistering day, the pale white stone felt cool against her fingers. *Think*, she told herself. *Think hard: How do we get out of the valley?* She felt her pulse race, and a rapid-fire slide show of images flashed through her mind so fast that she gasped.

A path, low and sandy; the sun cut in half by a high ridge; a man in robes; a dark gap in light stone . . .

She released the amulet, overwhelmed.

"What did you see?" said Alex, leaning in.

How could she explain it to him? How could she tell him the simple truth: *I don't know.*

"Too much," she said. "And not enough."

His expression sank. Even Luke, standing next to him, made a stink face. She always worked so hard to have all the answers, and now all this stupid amulet did was give her questions. Unless . . . "Maybe I know which way to go, though?" she said, remembering the first image, the path.

"Really?" said Alex.

The sun beat down on her. She felt like she was being baked. *Focus, Ren!* She concentrated on the second image. "We need to follow a path and then head up the ridge," she said.

"Okay," said Alex, desperation growing in his voice. "But which way? This place is full of paths."

Ren thought hard. If they went in the wrong direction, they were fried. She'd seen the sun cut in half by the ridgeline in her vision. It had been rising. "East," she said, pointing toward the morning sun.

"You're sure?" said Luke. His face was bright red beneath his cap.

She nodded. They needed to move, and it was the best she had. "We need to find a higher ridgeline." At least they were headed in the same direction the taxi had gone.

They moved along the valley floor as fast as they could in the punishing heat, looking up occasionally to size up the ridge above them. They stayed off the little road and followed a winding path that hugged the base of one of the limestone cliffs that formed the edge of the valley. The morning sun was still low enough that the ridgeline above them offered some shade.

Still, the temperature was climbing steadily. Ren felt her body temperature rising, too. It was like she had a fever inside and out.

She looked at the others: Alex in his silly hat, Luke in his cap, both pouring sweat, leaning forward as they marched grimly along.

We won't last long, she thought.

"I feel trapped down here," muttered Luke.

Alex nodded. "When the sun comes over that ridge, we'll be baked alive," he said.

"We need to get out!" said Luke. He veered to the side and scrambled up the valley wall.

But the combination of hard stone and shifting sand made climbing too hard, and Ren watched as he slid back down to where he started.

Alex turned to her. "Does *any* of this look familiar?" he said.

His voice was pleading, desperate. Ren looked out at the path in front of them and up at the ridge. When it came right down to it, one desert path looks a lot like another. So did one rocky ridge. Her earlier confidence evaporated, and for a moment she wished she'd never found the ibis. She peered into the distance again. She saw a wall of wavy heat haze rising from a dark strip of road running along the sun-blasted valley floor. She followed it with her eyes.

"Is that a little building?" she said.

The others whipped their heads around.

"Maybe it has AC!" said Luke, taking off at a run. Alex

followed. Ren refused to run after them. It was just a little hut on the side of the road. It didn't have air conditioning. Where would it even get the electricity?

She arrived just in time to see Alex and Luke rushing back out of what she now realized was a one-room guard booth or checkpoint, maybe both. She saw the familiar logo of the Supreme Council painted on the side, white paint on red, all of it peeling from the heat.

"Any cooler inside?" she asked, knowing the answer.

"It's like an oven!" said Alex, stuffing something square and plastic into his backpack.

"Is that a binder?" said Ren, a bit of an expert on the subject.

"It's the visitor log," he said. "From the guard booth."

The group left the little red oven behind and trudged on, deeper into the deep fryer. The sliver of shadow shrank, forcing them closer and closer to the valley wall. But then . . .

"Let's ask him how to get out!" said Alex, pointing.

Ren followed his finger and couldn't believe it. There was a man walking toward them. He was out in the open sunlight and his entire bottom half was obscured by the heat haze. But one thing was clear: He was wearing loose-fitting desert robes — just like the man the ibis had shown her.

"Hey!" called Ren.

"Dude!" called Luke.

The man adjusted his course immediately, turning to head toward them. And for just a second, Ren had a bad feeling.

The man's head was wrapped in white cloth, with just a narrow gap for his eyes. *Was he a desert tribesman?* wondered Ren. *A nomad?* She'd read about them, how they could survive in even the harshest conditions.

His robes were loose and lightweight. Their light color matched the sand, and she could see how they might offer some protection from the brutal heat. The man was no more than ten feet away now.

"Hello!" Alex called with as much cheer as he could muster.

Ren searched the man's eyes for any sign of kindness or understanding and found none. Alex must have seen the same thing, because she saw him take hold of his amulet.

Now the man did speak — a handful of words — but Ren didn't understand the language. Alex replied, and she couldn't understand that, either. She'd seen this before. The amulet was allowing him to speak ancient Egyptian. *But that meant . . .*

Before she could finish her thought, the man stepped into the shadow cast by the ridge, and everything about him changed. His loose clothing shimmered and faded away, gone just like the heat haze that had surrounded him. In its place, an ancient outfit: a white tunic laced with golden thread, a white kilt of similar material, sandals on his feet. And on his head: an ornate headdress. The face beneath it was dark tan, the color of a fawn's fur, and horribly blistered.

Now Ren knew exactly what they were facing — and how much trouble they were in.

"Holy —" began Luke, but before he got any further, a pulse of pure white light flashed out from the man's eyes. All three friends called out in pain and surprise. Every inch of exposed skin had been suddenly and severely sunburned, but they had a bigger problem. Ren blinked, testing.

She was blind.

"Death Walker!" Alex shouted. Ren cupped her hands over her light-stung eyes. All she could see were swirls of yellow and orange.

"Run!" called Alex. "Follow my voice!"

But the first thing Ren heard was Alex tripping and falling heavily to the ground.

Ren turned and tried to run. She made it five steps before her boot caught on some unseen edge and sent her sprawling. The hard-packed, sunbaked ground scraped her palms.

She felt a whoosh of air and knew it was Luke rushing past, faster and more coordinated by a mile. She scrambled to her feet as her eyes began to clear.

She turned and squinted at the man. He was standing with his head tilted toward the sky and his arms raised above him. In between his outstretched hands — and in between the pinpricks of light dotting her vision — she saw a roiling ball of fire. The flames swirled in a circle and licked outward greedily. She could feel the heat of the thing on her face.

The swirling ball of flames grew larger, and the man's face tilted down toward the spot where she stood transfixed, hypnotized by the liquid fire. Her feet wouldn't move, but her mind was racing back toward the piled bones in the tomb. She knew all too well that Death Walkers fed on souls, and now she understood that this one preferred hot meals.

He smiled as he saw the horror dawn on her face.

He pulled his arms back. When his arms came forward, so would the flames.

Alex's eyes were dazzled, his knees were skinned, and his left hand was wrapped so hard around his scarab that its wings threatened to punch right through the skin of his palm. Once again, the Death Walker spoke, shouting the same question he had asked before: "Little children, who do you worship?"

Alex knew that ancient Egyptians could be very particular about their many gods, but he had a more pressing question in mind: *How do you stop a walking undead flamethrower?*

As the Walker's fierce, predatory eyes focused on Ren, as his arms swung back like a pitcher about to deliver some high heat, Alex swept his free hand back and swiftly forward.

The wind that comes before the rain . . . His amulet had desert magic, and they were in the desert now. A wind more powerful than Alex expected rose instantly and swept across the floor of the valley. Alex braced himself as it rushed past, nearly toppling him. The wind carried with it a swirling, stabbing sea of sand. He felt a thousand sharp stings against his exposed arms. His hat flew off and forward, and now he felt the stings against his neck and cheeks, too.

Scraped up off the valley floor and carried along, the sand was so thick that it seemed to block out the sun itself. The world turned tan and then almost black. Alex saw the glow of the flaming orb smothered completely. As it blinked out, he closed his eyes against the stinging tumult.

A moment later, it was over. The sand and wind had passed. Alex opened his eyes to find Ren hunched over on the ground, hands shielding her head. Luke was a little farther back, bent over, spitting out sand. The Death Walker had dropped to one knee, his headdress slightly askew.

He looked up, and Alex's breath caught. Sand clung to the Walker's face, wet from the oozing blisters, and he glared at his enemy with eyes that were now glowing red.

"RUN!" called Alex.

They rushed past the Walker as he slowly rose to his feet. They gave him a wide berth — except for Luke, who shouldered directly into him. There was a sizzling sound as he made contact.

"Aaah!" cried Luke.

But the impact had done its job, knocking the Walker back to the ground.

Injured or not, Luke ran like a gazelle. "Are you okay?" shouted Alex as his cousin quickly caught up.

"No!" shouted Luke. "Felt like tackling a campfire."

After a few more strides, Alex risked a quick look back. The Death Walker was on his feet now. His hands were raised above him, and in between them, a ball of flame was forming. Alex kicked it up a gear, still amazed at his new health, still testing its limits. It was torture to run in this heat, but crazy desperation fueled him. His body responded, his engine revved, but at any second he expected it all to end in flames.

He'd caught the Walker off guard. He knew it wouldn't work again. By the time he turned and faced him, he'd be a pile of ash and bone.

Alex searched for some escape, but to their left, the limestone face of the valley wall rose steeply. To their right, the ground was exposed and bathed in brutal sun.

"Over here!" said Ren, already veering toward the base of the slope.

"Why?" he shouted in between gasps for air. "Where?"

But now he saw it: a gap in between two jutting wedges of limestone. The opening was narrow, barely as wide as he was, but the darkness within hinted at depth. "Is that a cave or —"

"Just go!" Luke shouted, passing him.

Alex heard a crackling sound growing behind him as he took a sharp left on the fly. A fireball whooshed past him.

He felt its searing heat as it passed, scalding his skin even though it missed.

The Death Walker roared his disapproval behind them — and the roar sounded close. A quick glance back confirmed it. He was rushing toward them at incredible speed, sandals slapping sand.

Alex turned to see Luke and Ren running for the crevice in the valley wall, just steps ahead of him. It was a thin slice of pure black cutting deep into the base of the slope. It could hold anything or nothing at all — and the friends hit it at a dead run.

Alex saw Ren disappear into the darkness.

And then Luke.

And then it was his turn. He closed his eyes and braced himself, expecting to run straight into the back of a cave, or at least his friends. Instead, he ran into a dark, narrow passage.

"This way!" Ren shouted from somewhere up ahead, her voice echoing off the limestone that surrounded them.

He followed the narrow, sloping passage: forward and up.

"Hurry!" he shouted, risking a quick look back at the wedge of light at the entrance. "He's right behind us."

Alex's heart hammered in his chest and his entire right side burned. The claustrophobic darkness raised his fear to near panic. His frantic mind could form only the most basic questions: *Where did this passage go? Were they just moving deeper into the mountain? Wedging themselves in?*

The sound of footsteps and hard, sharp breaths filled the narrow stone gap at first, but soon another sound rose up. A crackling sound, like a thousand insects feeding.

"Go, go, go!" called Alex from the end of the line.

Up ahead, Ren finally managed to wrestle the flashlight free from her pack. She clicked it on just in time to avoid running into the wall at a sharp bend in the passageway.

She swung around the corner, then Luke. Alex thrust his left hand out to avoid crashing into the wall as he made the sharp turn to the right. The fireball hit the wall a split-second later.

Flames licked around the corner, and the passageway lit up and filled with a wave of heat that nearly buckled Alex's knees. But the thing had extinguished itself on the wall.

And now there was light up ahead. Not fire, but sunlight.

The friends made for the opening as fast as they could, but their heavy legs and overheated systems couldn't manage more than a jog. Ren stumbled out first. Then Luke. Alex took one last look back, but all he saw was gray smoke curling in the darkness.

He turned and burst into sunlight. Ren and Luke were bent over with their hands on their knees on the slope of the ridge, balanced on a small ledge that protruded like a lower lip under the cave's open mouth. The valley spread out below them. Luke stuck out his arm to prevent Alex from toppling off it.

Alex nodded his thanks, then bent over and coughed

smoke out of his lungs. He looked up, trying to gauge the distance to the top of the ridge.

"Look at this," said Luke. "I think it's a path."

Alex looked and would have pumped his fist if he'd had the energy. An old footpath led upward from the ledge, cutting back and forth across the face of the slope, leading toward the top of the ridge and out of the valley. Alex looked back at the passage and understood: a secret escape route for the tomb raiders that pillaged the valley in ancient times. Tired, overheated, burned, thirsty, and cramping badly in his side, Alex fell into line behind the other two and followed the path as best he could. "How did you know that cave would save us?" he said to Ren's back once he had some fresh air back in his lungs.

"I didn't, really," said Ren. "But I was hoping it wouldn't try to kill me twice."

Alex wasn't really sure what she meant, but the climb was too tough for follow-up questions or complicated answers. Instead, he kept his feet moving and his eyes peeled. There was no sign of the Walker on the slope below them, but there was trouble above. The rising sun was eating away at the last of the shade. The heat was unforgiving as they climbed. They trudged on, bent over and silent except for their labored breathing, until eventually they made it.

At some point during the climb, he'd passed Ren. Now he reached back and tugged her over the top of the ridge with him. Luke was already collapsed on the ground. The air was instantly cooler on the other side. Even the direct heat of the desert sun paled in comparison to the supernatural sauna of the valley itself. For maybe a minute, all they did was lie on their backs and breathe.

Luke dug his water bottle out of his pack, took a swig, and then passed the bottle to his cousin.

It was the best thing Alex had ever tasted. He took two greedy gulps, wiped his mouth, and passed the bottle to Ren. She took a sustained gulp that would have made a camel proud.

"You were hoping what wouldn't try to kill you twice?" said Alex, finally picking up the question he'd let drop on the climb. "The Death Walker?"

Ren looked up into the bright blue sky and shook her head. "My amulet," she said.

A Visitor in the Night

Darkness had fallen. The temperature had dropped, but Alex could still feel the heat radiating off his skin on the side the Death Walker's fireball had passed. Luke had blisters where he'd touched the Walker. And Ren was just as sunburned as the rest of them from the blinding blast of light.

They sat in front of the small fire they'd built, moving as little as possible. Everything hurt. "I need, like, some lotion or something," said Luke, poking at a blister near his elbow.

He was sitting in a folding chair. Along with a small stack of dried-out firewood, also currently in use, the chair was the only thing that had been left of the tomb robbers' campsite. After being caught hammer-handed, Alex figured the secretive crooks had sought out an even more remote hideout.

"This whole thing was a trap," moaned Ren, keeping the complaint ball rolling. "Hesaan knew there was a Death Walker here, and he sent us right to it . . ."

"Explains why there was someone on the train here, too," offered Luke.

Alex barely heard them. He was too busy scouring the visitor's log he'd taken from the council's guard booth. The plastic cover was partially melted, and the pages inside were dried and crisp. They reminded Alex of ancient papyrus, and they might as well have been.

He turned to the next page and tipped it toward the glow of the fire. Once again, he was confronted with row after row of scrawled names and dates. Most of the entries were in Arabic, but he concentrated on the English entries. There was one column for printed names, another for signatures, and another for what must have been reason for visit. The occasional date in English told him he was in the right range . . .

"Well, whatever," said Ren. "Because they sent the wrong three kids into this trap. *We* know what to do with a Death Walker."

Luke sat back and released a *do we have to* groan, and Alex looked up from his logbook.

"This thing is *killing people*, Luke," Ren continued. "We need to get the Book of the Dead. I'll bet there's one in Luxor. And we need to figure out who this Death Walker is, so we know which spell to use against him."

Alex looked at the fire and blinked a few times, trying to reset his eyes after too much dim-light reading. He was sure there was something going on in Tut's tomb. The bones, the burned Aten . . . But most of all, the feeling he'd gotten from his amulet. It wouldn't light up like that for nothing. It had to be something big. And if it was the Spells, hidden somewhere inside there . . .

"Okay," he said. This time he was the tie-breaker. "We need to go back to KV 62, and we can't go back into the valley without some way to fight that guy."

"What we need to do is not get burned to bacon," said Luke.

"We should head into Luxor first thing tomorrow," said Ren. "We can't fight a Death Walker without the Book of the Dead."

Alex couldn't focus on Luxor, though — his thoughts were still in the desert. "I think the Spells really might be down there. The scarab went crazy in that tomb . . . Maybe my mom really was just putting them back, to keep them safe." He liked the idea. It explained why she was doing it on her own, in secret. It was kind of noble, even. But the others looked skeptical.

"Do you really think they're there?" said Ren. "We went through that tomb."

Cheered up by his new theory, Alex managed a small smile. He lowered his sunburned face toward the firelight: "I definitely think we're getting warmer . . ."

The sound of soft laughter spilled like much-needed rain into the desert night.

But just as Alex was reaching down to pick up the logbook again, he heard something.

"Shhh!" he said. "What was that?"

The other two froze.

Tsss–tsss–tsss–tsss.

Such a small sound, like someone stabbing a sack of flour with a small, sharp blade . . .

"I hear it," whispered Ren, her eyes opening wide. "It's coming from . . ." She turned and pointed, just as the source of the noise entered the glow of the dying fire. "It's Pai again," said Ren.

"Mmmur-rack?" said the mummy cat.

Luke eyed her uneasily. "No burger," he noted.

Ren stayed seated in the sand and tried to coax Pai-en-Inmar, sacred servant of Bastet, into her lap. "She makes me feel safe."

A voice sounded from the opposite side of the fire, clear and almost singsong, but in an ancient language.

All three human heads swung around frantically, and even Pai ventured a look over her shoulder.

Luke tipped backward in his chair, arms windmilling wildly as he spilled onto the ground. "Gah!" he said, desperately scrambling to his feet. "Who is it? Is it the Walker?"

"I don't understand this one," said the figure, gesturing toward Luke.

Alex had wrapped his hand around his amulet out of sheer survival instinct. He understood the words, but it took him a moment to muster a response.

"I know you," he managed finally, staring up from his spot by the fire.

"You, I understand," said the figure, taking another step into the light. He seemed to consider it for a moment and then turned his hand palm up and raised it a few inches. "You may rise, my subjects."

Alex and Ren slowly stood, and Luke followed a few beats later.

Alex looked down. "You . . . you have feet."

The young man looked to be no more than eighteen, with bronze skin and handsome, somehow familiar features. He was wrapped in ornate robes and looking down at his own feet. "So I do," he said, "but I never liked these sandals."

His sandaled feet were bare, just like his head and hands, but a band of tightly wrapped linen was visible below the hem of his robes. Alex looked closer and saw scraps of linen peeking out from the wrists and neck of the garments as well.

The figure looked up and met Alex's stare. Alex wasn't trying to be rude, he just couldn't quite believe it. He recognized the face, of course. It looked exactly like the most famous gold funerary mask in history.

"Tutankhamun," he said in a hushed, reverent tone.

"Yes," said the boy king, "but you may call me Pharaoh or Supreme Ruler or Almighty Emissary of the Great and Powerful Amun-Re. Whatever makes you comfortable."

"King Tut?" said Ren, incredulous.

"Yes," he said, shrugging. "I suppose that will do, too."

Alex looked over at Ren and saw her look down at the spot where her left hand encircled her ibis. Ren was speaking ancient Egyptian, too.

"Duuuuuude!" said Luke, pointing at Tut. "You're famous!"

Tut stared at him blankly, and then turned to Alex. "What is the meaning of *Duuuuuude*? Is that this strange boy's name?"

Alex glanced over at his cousin. "Kind of," he said.

"I see," said Tut. "But I grow weary of you all. I will pet your cat now, as is my divine right."

But Pai seemed unconvinced.

Tut took one step closer and Pai backed up.

A second step and she hissed.

"Perhaps not," said Tut, changing course. "I would hate to get scratched." He looked down at Pai. "Fine, you little beast," he said. "Flea receptacle. All I did was restore the worship of the old gods, your master included. All I did was rebuild their temples. Go ahead and hiss!"

Tut headed toward Luke, who backed up, but not fast enough to prevent the boy king from plucking the Yankees cap off his head.

"Hey!" said Luke. Tut ignored him and his dramatic hat head and turned back toward the other two. Holding the cap in one long elegant hand, he gestured toward the intertwined NY symbol with the other. "I am not familiar with this hieroglyph," he said. "What does it mean?"

"Some people call it the Evil Empire," said Alex, Mets fan to the core.

"Mmmm," said Tut. "I am familiar with those."

"What, uh, what are you doing here?" said Alex, before quickly adding: "Your, um, majesty?"

Tut considered him for a second, taking in his stained clothes and burned skin with a look of mild disdain. "I saw the fire," he said. He dropped the cap in the sand and began walking away. "And anyway," he added. "I am looking for something."

Without another word, he disappeared into the night to continue his search.

Going to Town

Alex, Ren, and Luke were all from New York City, so they'd had their share of celebrity sightings. But those celebs had all been alive.

Talking about Tut gave them some energy as they made their way through the Egyptian morning toward the first ferry to Luxor.

"He was kind of full of himself," said Luke. "Total diva."

"Pharaohs were told they were living gods," said Alex sleepily. "I could see that going to your head."

"Yeah, but he just, like, dropped my hat."

Alex shrugged. "It *is* a Yankees cap."

Luke blew air out his nose. "Please," he said. "The Mets are doormats. How are we even related?"

"He was kind of handsome, though," offered Ren.

Now Alex blew air out of his nose. "He wasn't really," he said. "I mean, not back then."

"No?" said Ren, a little disappointment in her voice.

"Nope," said Alex triumphantly. "He was a scrawny,

buck-toothed little dude. I saw a show where they recon-structed what he looked like from X-rays and stuff."

"Nerd," said Luke. "Mets nerd."

"Well, he didn't look scrawny last night," said Ren.

Luke agreed. "Dude was ripped."

"Yeah, he looked just like his funeral mask," said Alex.

"Right," said Ren. She knew this one. "The ancient Egyptians believed that if they had a statue of themselves built before they died, they could, like, inhabit it in the afterlife. Their spirit could take on its shape. Remember how the last Death Walker looked just like his statue? Tut looks like his mask."

"Bigger nerd," said Luke. "Non-baseball nerd." But then he had another thought. "I'd build my statue twenty feet tall!"

They turned a corner and the Nile came into view below them, a broad black ribbon in the soft morning light.

Inside the ferry, the crew outnumbered the passengers. The burned and blistering friends took their seats stiffly. They leaned in and counted how much money they had left after buying their ferry tickets. Medicine was liable to be expensive.

"When we call Todtman, we can ask him to send more," said Alex.

"Or maybe bring it with him," said Ren. "Now that we know what we're dealing with here, he'll probably want to come help out."

Alex hoped he'd come. Todtman would give them a lot more firepower.

As they settled in for the rest of the trip, Alex pulled out the binder.

"Aren't you done with that yet?" said Ren.

"It was hard to read by one little campfire," he protested. "I could barely . . ." But as his eyes fell on the next line, he realized that he was done after all. He stopped speaking and even stopped breathing for a while.

"What?" said Ren, scooting around on the bench seat for a look.

Alex pointed to an entry halfway down the page, written in dull pencil. Ren leaned in. "Who's Angela Felini?"

"She was my babysitter," said Alex, "in third grade."

"You mean Angie? Angie with the ponytail? She was your favorite!"

Alex nodded. "My mom's, too." He stabbed the crinkly page with his finger. "And that's my mom's handwriting."

"So wait," said Luke. "Was your babysitter here or not?"

Alex shook his head absently. He was staring at the last column, after the scrawled — and faked — signature. Reason for visit: "Leaving valley."

"Look at the date," said Ren, but Alex already had.

His mom was gone. As sure as Angela Felini had moved to Alexandria, Virginia, Maggie Bauer had been stopped at the checkpoint on the way out of the valley seven days earlier, signed a fake name — and disappeared. He stared at the familiar handwriting. How many notes had he seen it on? How many birthday cards?

"At least we know for sure," said Ren, patting him on the shoulder. "She was here. Now we need to know if she left anything behind."

Alex knew she meant the Spells, and he knew she was right. But he was caught up on new question: *Why that name? Was it just the first one she'd thought of . . . or a message?*

They called Todtman from just outside a little riverside teahouse as soon as they got off the boat. The call went straight to voice mail.

"We're in Luxor," said Alex. "Call us today, please." He paused as two men walked by, one walking into the teahouse, the other walking out. "We found something, and . . . something found us. It's important. Call us back. Okay, um, bye."

"Why didn't he answer?" said Ren.

"It's still early," said Alex. "He'll call back."

They headed toward the main drag of the city. The remote desert ridge had seemed to offer protection from The Order, but now they were back out in the open, and Alex felt exposed and vulnerable. And almost immediately, they caught sight of some commotion. A small crowd had gathered near the entrance to the Temple of Luxor.

Alex's mouth was full of one of the rubbery buttered rolls they'd bought at the tea place, so he looked at the others and raised his eyebrows.

"Let's check it out," said Ren, who'd eaten her roll like a vacuum cleaner.

As they drew closer, they saw a crane lowering a massive stone block onto an oversized flatbed truck.

"They're taking the stones right from the dromos," said Alex, his tone distant with disbelief.

"From the what?" said Luke.

Alex pointed to the monument-lined path that led from Luxor Temple to Karnak. "Those," said Alex, "are some seriously sacred stones."

Alex's jaw dropped as the crane plucked another massive block free and hoisted it toward the back of the truck. A ram-headed sphinx statue that had ridden high atop the stone for thousands of years now sat forlornly on the ground, bearing silent witness. The crowd jeered and pushed forward. One of the city's biggest tourist attractions was being dismantled before their eyes.

And that's when Alex saw the guards. Half a dozen men took a step toward the crowd, which instantly shrank back. Alex had originally mistaken them for workers, but that was before he saw the pistols in their hands. The men were wearing matching khaki uniforms, but there were no insignias. They weren't army or police.

So where are the police? Alex searched the crowd and found Ren one step ahead of him. "Why don't you stop them?" she was saying to a pair of police officers standing, arms folded, at the edge of the crowd.

Alex rushed over. The first officer just shook his head, not understanding, but the second spoke English well. "The papers *seem* to be in order," he said. "From the government . . ."

From the way he said "seem to be," Alex knew he didn't

believe it. And from the grim expressions on their faces, he knew that neither of them much liked it.

Puhh-WHUMMMPP!

Alex swung around as the massive stone block was lowered onto the back of the truck. There were already four others on there, and the huge vehicle's entire frame seemed to bend and slump under the weight.

On the other side of the crane, yelling something at its operator, was a woman whose crisp suit hung loosely on her almost skeletal frame.

Peshwar.

"Ren! Luke!" he yelped, and motioned them quickly back into the crowd.

"Peshwar's here," he said.

"So The Order's doing this?" Ren asked nervously. Alex could see her turning the pieces over in her head. "Why does The Order need a bunch of huge rocks?"

The big truck started up and the crowd jeered again as two plumes of black smoke belched from its exhaust pipes.

"Not rocks," said Alex. "Sacred stones." But he still didn't know why they'd want them. He turned to watch as the truck pulled away, loaded with the blocks, heavy and strong. *Did the ancient stones hold some power?*

A few men tried to get in front of the truck as it pulled away. A warning shot was fired in the air. There were angry shouts, but in the end, the men moved and the crowd dispersed. The friends disappeared with it, slipping onto a side street.

Missing Mummies

"I feel sticky," said Ren.

"Are you sure this stuff is medicine and not toothpaste?" said Luke. He pulled the tube they'd just purchased out of his pack and squinted at the label, as if narrowing his eyes would somehow transform the Arabic alphabet.

"Pretty sure?" said Ren, flapping her guidebook and its glossary of Arabic terms in his general direction.

"I think it's working," said Alex. "My neck feels a little better."

"Yeah," said Luke, looking down at the angry red skin on his upper arm. "At least my bicep won't get any cavities."

They stayed close to the buildings and did their best to keep out of sight. The lioness was in the city, but there was no way they were leaving until they'd found clues to the Death Walker's identity, and a copy of the Book of the Dead. They headed down a street called Corniche el-Nile toward their first destination, Luxor's famous Mummification Museum.

"Wait, I've got to call home," said Luke as they passed a quiet stretch of small, seemingly deserted buildings. "It's been days." He pulled out his phone and disappeared around the corner of one of the buildings.

He came back a few minutes later looking pale, which was impressive considering his sunburn. Alex gave him a *What's up?* look. Luke looked down and avoided his eyes. "I'm in serious trouble," he said.

Alex got the point. He knew it was a tenuous web of excuses and cover stories that allowed them to be here at all. Luke's parents thought he was still at a sports camp in London — at least they had — and Ren's parents thought she was still on a summer internship at the British Museum — at least he hoped.

"I should call, too," Ren said.

Alex thought it could wait, but he didn't say so. He knew Ren was homesick. The other two waited as she disappeared into the alleyway-turned-phone booth. She returned a few minutes later, looking like her call had gone better than Luke's — or Alex's still unreturned call to Todtman. She flipped her guidebook open for one last look at the map. "We're just a few blocks away now," she said.

A minute later, they walked down a flight of broad white stairs to enter the museum. *Of course it's underground*, thought Alex.

⟨—+——+——+—⟩

The mummy museum was operating with a skeleton crew.

As near as Ren could tell it was just two guys. The younger one took their money at the door.

"Here are your tickets," he said in a thick French accent. *"Merci."*

Once he was out of earshot, they got down to business. "We're looking for the Book, but also missing mummies," whispered Alex.

"Why are we looking for mummies in town when there's a valley full of tombs out there?" said Luke, his tone somewhere between annoyed and defeated.

"The Valley of the Kings has been heavily excavated," whispered Alex. "The important mummies were really coveted. A lot of them are in museums here. If we can find out which ones have gone walking, it might give us a clue to the Death Walker's identity. We need to know who he was in life so we know which spell will work on him now."

Luke knew that part already but barely managed half a nod. Ren could tell he was still upset. She walked a little closer. "Is it your parents?" she said.

"Yeah," he said. "Kind of."

"Bummer," she said, taking out her pen. Her own hadn't caught on yet. They were still watching the British Broadcasting Corporation news every night, as if they might catch sight of her — and it had been nice to talk to them.

They searched the sleepy museum.

The Frenchman shadowed them discretely for the first

few rooms. He faded away after he saw that they were on their best museum behavior.

In the next room, they caught their first glimpse of the Book of the Dead.

"Here's some of it," said Alex, lifting his chin toward the mummy in front of him.

"Where?" said Ren.

"On the wrappings."

She looked closely. The ink was faded and the linen had gone brown with age, but now she saw it: neat rows of hieroglyphic symbols leading to tiny paintings. She recognized the depiction of the weighing of the heart ceremony by now: There was the scale with a heart on one side and a feather on the other. The god Thoth stood by to record the result: Would the heart be weighed down by guilt and be destroyed forever?

Thoth had the head of an ibis. *For this guy's sake*, she thought, looking over at the mummy, *I hope that ibis is more reliable than mine.* She didn't understand why her amulet was failing her so often. She tried so hard every time she used it . . .

"I hope you don't expect us to cart this dude out of here," she whispered to Alex.

"No," he said. "It's just a few spells anyway. And we still don't know which one we need."

Ren nodded. In London, they'd used a spell of protection against grave robbers to banish a Walker who'd been a notorious tomb raider. The right missing mummy could tell them who this Death Walker was — and what spell to use against him. They had more luck with that search. Three of the museum's mummy exhibits were hidden under solemn tents of black cloth, as if camping out in the afterlife.

"Do you think they're gone?" said Ren. "Or they're just moving around under there?" They'd seen two mummies moving at the Met: a little girl twisting in her open coffin, and the Stung Man, climbing out of his.

"Dunno," said Alex, but that was before he took hold of his amulet.

His eyes turned black, windows onto a world that made Ren shiver, and she looked away.

"Gone," he said, the white and brown returning to his eyes as he released the scarab. "All three."

Is one of these missing mummies the Death Walker? Ren walked around and wrote down the info on each in her ever-present notebook. The information plaque by the first one said:

KHAEMKHEMWY, NOBLEMAN, DIED CIRCA 2217 BC

The second one was a priest:

AKHENOTRA, ROYAL PRIEST IN THE COURT OF THE PHARAOH AKHENATEN, DIED CIRCA 1319 BC

"This one's young!" she said, when she came to the third plaque. "Died around 100 BC."

Luke pulled his eyes up off the floor and scanned the plaque. "Wealthy desert trader," he said. "Bet that dude rocked some robes."

125

Ren remembered the Walker's appearance as he approached them across the sandy terrain. She wrote down the name, Thetan-Ankh, and underlined it twice.

They took one more look around the small museum, but all the other mummies still seemed to be present — and dead. They were nearly back where they started before she saw it: another weighing of the heart ceremony. But the heart in this painting was so tiny that it was more like the weighing of a flea.

Alex turned to look where Ren was pointing and his eyes opened wide. "Is that the whole thing?" he said, eyeing the two flattened scrolls. Each was mounted on a board no more than two feet wide.

Ren was already leaning in to read the information plaque under the glass case. "The Book of the Dead of Hebsany," it read. "Hebsany was a wealthy scribe who gained fame for his skill as a draughtsman and copyist. Given his profession, it is likely that he prepared his own Book of the Dead. It remains the smallest complete copy ever found."

"Complete!" Ren jumped back — and bumped into Alex, who was reading over her shoulder. "Watch it!" she said.

He put one finger up to his lips and shushed her. "It's perfect," he whispered, and right away she knew he meant to take it.

"How?" she mouthed.

Alex nodded down toward his amulet. "If I can get the case open without setting off any alarms, I can just stack the boards and put them in my pack . . ."

Ren and Luke both instinctively glanced across the room. The entrance was just through the door, and they could hear the muffled conversation of the two museum workers.

Ren thought about it. "I can handle the guards," she said. "Just be careful — and hurry."

Then she turned sharply on the heel of her boot and strode out into the entrance room. *"Bonjour!"* she said brightly. *"Mon nom est Ren!"*

Her French wasn't the greatest, she knew, but what better reason to practice? She just hoped she didn't end up completing the lesson in jail.

There was a loud *plonk* from the next room. The Frenchman shot his *petit inquisiteur* a sharp look and strode past her. She fired questions at his back: *"Comment allez-vous? Où sont les toilettes?"*

As he was about to round the corner into the room, Alex and Luke came marching out. "Oh, there you are, Ren!" said Alex. She wondered if anyone else noticed the thin layer of sweat on his forehead. "We were looking for you. Well, time to go!"

"Thanks, dudes," said Luke as the three friends filed out the front door. "Sweet museum."

The two men gave them small waves and slightly baffled looks. Ren was halfway up the stairs to the street when she heard the door fly open behind them. The friends broke into a run as the men shouted for them to stop.

Betrayed

Losing two museum workers on the tricky side streets of the old city wasn't that big a challenge. For kids used to battling the undead, the merely out of shape proved easy. The friends headed straight for the ferry, and from there to a taxi to the Valley of the Kings.

They rode fast and with the windows down, the warm wind whipping through the boxy car. Alex's thoughts were just as turbulent, and he sat in the front seat just to be a few feet closer to their destination. He remembered the hot buzz of his amulet in the tomb, the carefully printed name from his past. It seemed like everyone and everything was trying to tell him something. He needed to know what!

He checked his phone one last time before they lost service. Nothing. *Why hadn't Todtman called?* Even the silence seemed telling. He pictured the old scholar, alone in the vipers' nest Cairo had become. The last bar vanished from his phone, and it felt like a door slamming between them.

The friends climbed out of the cab a hundred yards from

the mouth of the valley, but the heat coming from it still hit Alex's face as if he'd opened the oven to check on a frozen pizza. Rather than getting an inch closer, the taxi backed up to turn around.

Once the friends were alone in the unforgiving desert, the weight of their mission hit them. They were quiet for a few long moments. They could die out here, and no one would know. "We'll have to wait till sunset to head into the valley to look for the Spells and destroy the Walker," said Alex at last. He looked up at the sun as Ren looked down at her watch. "Let's head back to camp and see if we can figure out which spell we need. Maybe we can use your amulet."

Ren looked at him like he was dense. "What?" he said. "It's a good idea."

Luke started heading up the slope for the long walk back to camp, and Ren turned and followed him. The sun was just beginning to set by the time they arrived. Alex had been worried that they might find the place ransacked. But he'd never expected this.

The most famous eighteen-year-old king in human history — dead some 3,300 years — sat in the saggy-bottomed nylon camp chair idly petting a mummy cat.

Luke raised his hands and looked at the sky: *What next?*

Ren eyed Pai, her loyalty suddenly in question.

Tut began to speak. It took Alex a few seconds to get his hand around his amulet, and he only caught the last few words: "no need to bow."

Alex hadn't planned on it, but it did raise the question: What exactly do you say to the earthly incarnation of a long-dead boy king?

"We, uh, we were at your place yesterday," he ventured.

Tut looked at him. With his sculpted features, he looked like a well-tanned boy band member, albeit one in robes and a funny hat. "That dump?" said Tut.

"Are you kidding?" said Alex. "It was full of the most famous treasure in the world!"

"There's no treasure there now," said Tut. "Just a few rooms and some sloppy paintings. Have you even seen Ramses's tomb? Magnificent!"

"Yours was done in a hurry, wasn't it?" said Alex.

Tut shifted uncomfortably in his seat. "Yes," he admitted. "Everyone was in a terrible rush after the murder."

"You really were murdered?" said Ren. Alex looked over and saw her grasping her amulet.

"I was betrayed," said Tut.

"But why?" said Ren. "You seem like such a . . ." She paused, fumbling for the rest of the sentence. ". . . good king?"

"She means a handsome king," said Alex.

Ren glared at him, but Tut took the exchange in stride. "I was both," he said. "But I made enemies."

"The sun cult that you abolished?" said Alex. "The one started by your father, Akhenaten."

"Yes," said Tut, wincing slightly at the memory. "Dad got a little . . . carried away with that. Banned the old gods, worshipped the sun — my whole childhood I was sunburned from praying to the thing. So, yes, I changed that right away. Brought back the old gods — and paid for it."

"What language are you all speaking, Goofball-ese?" said Luke, taking a seat in the sand.

Ren, who now spoke impeccable New Kingdom Goofball, tried to explain it all to Luke. "Tut's father was pharaoh before him. He abolished the old religion — Amun-Re, Horus, Anubis, those guys — and created a new one. Tut brought the old gods back when he, like, took over. And then he was killed for it."

"Hey, Ren," said Alex, lifting the scarab slightly from his chest and lifting his chin toward her ibis. "Pretty cool, huh?"

"Yeah," admitted Ren. "I guess."

"Yes," confirmed Tut, thinking they were talking about him rather than their amulets' translation abilities. "I am that, too."

Alex had a few things he'd been hoping to ask Tut, and now seemed like the time. "Do you know anything about the Lost Spells?" he began. "Or a Death —"

"You know," interrupted Tut, slightly annoyed. "I am usually the one asking the questions. If you had —" But this time he was the one interrupted, by a cat. Pai made a sudden leap out of Tut's lap and headed toward Ren.

"Betrayed again," said Tut as he watched the freaky feline pad across the sand.

Ren knelt down to greet her, but the mummy cat slid right past her. They all turned to watch as Pai sat down and stared into the distance. Her tail began to flick back and forth in a quick, agitated way. She looked like a tabby cat watching sparrows through a window.

"She sees something," said Ren.

Alex tried to follow her gaze, but all he saw was the darkness gathering at the base of the slope. He suddenly got a bad feeling. "Maybe you'd better get the binoculars," he said.

Pai was still staring in the same direction when Ren returned. There was something there all right. Pai released a long, low *hisssssss*.

"We should get out of here," said Luke, standing suddenly and brushing the sand from his legs.

"What do you mean?" said Alex, but Luke didn't answer.

Ren was adjusting the knob of the binoculars and pointing it down the slope. They were all waiting for her verdict. Even Tutankhamun seemed to be leaning forward slightly in his modest nylon throne.

"Oh no," she whispered softly, as if all the air had just been knocked from her lungs.

"What is it?" said Alex, his own fear spiking at the dread in her voice.

"We need to go," she said, holding out the binoculars.

Alex took them and pointed them down the slope.

The day was dying and the sun was half hidden behind the ridge now, but even in the dim glow that remained, the clean white bone of the skull stood out. Pai hadn't spotted birds; she'd spotted another cat.

As Alex peered through the lenses, he saw the gaping eyeholes of the lioness skull peering back at him. Shapes shifted behind her. Alex struggled to refocus the binoculars with shaking hands. Half a dozen men, rifles slung over their shoulders, the barrels rising and falling with each step.

"They're coming for us," he said.

The group was marching directly up the slope. Alex looked around. Their campsite was tucked into a shady notch on a remote ridge, nearly invisible from a distance, and yet their pursuers seemed to know exactly where to go.

He looked at those around him, living and dead. They were far from Cairo now, far from Hesaan and whispers in the night . . .

Tut said something behind him. Alex had let go of his scarab and couldn't understand the words, but he was pretty sure he knew what Tut was asking. Alex grasped his amulet to answer.

"It's a hunting party," he said. "It looks like you're not the only one who's been betrayed."

Tut rose from his throne. "Well," he said. "That sounds horrible. I have no interest in being hunted — again." He began walking away, in the opposite direction from the one he'd taken the night before. "And I still have so much ground to search."

"What are you looking for anyway?" said Ren as he passed.

"A little piece of me," Tut said cryptically.

"Dude's got the right idea," said Luke as Tut headed away along the ridge.

Alex nodded. "We need to go. They're moving fast."

"But how did they know we were here?" said Ren.

"What does it matter?" said Luke, the strain evident in his usually chill voice.

They grabbed their small packs and hesitated. "Where are we going to go?" whispered Ren.

Alex paused. Could they risk the valley? The sun was low enough that they wouldn't be crisped, but they still hadn't figured out what spell to use if they ran into the Death Walker. It was too risky. They'd have to head down the slope and away from Peshwar.

But then Alex looked in that direction, and his heart sank.

It was hard to see the shapes in the dusk, but he could see the movement — and the rifle barrels caught the fading light well. More men, coming from the other direction. They were cut off.

"We have to head into the valley," Alex said, starting to scramble up to the top of the ridge. The last of the daylight bled away as they climbed.

"I don't like this!" said Ren. "We're not ready."

"I don't, either," said Alex, "but we don't have a choice. There are too many of them on this side —"

"Maybe we could lose them in the dark," said Luke.

Alex pictured Peshwar, those gaping eyeholes. He didn't know much about lions, but he knew cats could see in the dark. "We can't lose *her*," he said. "But maybe we'll be safe in the valley. Maybe they won't follow us."

"Of course they will!" said Ren.

Alex was getting frustrated. It was hard to argue and climb at the same time, and he didn't see what choice they had. "All right, so where do you want to go?"

His question was answered not by Ren but by a rifle. A far-off crack turned into a nearby snap as a bullet crashed into the stony ground at their feet. The Order men were well equipped — and in range.

The time for discussion was over. The friends reached the top of the ridge and paused for one fateful moment on the precipice. Another rifle crack pushed them on.

Pursued like animals under a darkening sky, they scrambled down into a valley of death.

The Dark Heart

Todtman's running days were over. He stood on a Cairo street corner, leaning on his jet-black walking stick. He had returned for one last look at the burned rubble of the building. Black smoke rose from the smoldering remains of old boards and older artifacts. Jinn had saved what he could, and now Todtman could only hope his friend would find safe haven elsewhere. His own possessions were lost; his cell phone no more than a mound of warped metal and molten plastic on the second floor.

Sirens sounded in the distance, just like the ones that had arrived far too late to save this building. Todtman saw a glow in the distance: another fire already blazing nearby. He didn't know if The Order had found his refuge, or if the dangers of the haunted city had merely caught up with him. He did know this: There would be no more safe shelter here. He had to act fast now, to "force the moment to its crisis," as his favorite poet had written.

He pivoted on his cane and headed into the night. The familiar click-clack was gone. Todtman looked down, pleased that something as simple as a circle of rubber on the tip of his cane could aid his mission.

He knew he would need all the help he could get as he headed into the dark heart of the city. He would find The Order headquarters this night, and he would do it not with the overworked eyes of an old man but with the timeless vision of a falcon. He had one hand free as he walked, and now he reached up and folded it around his amulet.

The location of The Order's headquarters in Cairo was a closely guarded secret, but its members were not hard to find. There was a café in the old city where they were said to conduct their business openly now, and Todtman turned in its direction. He knew the city well, and that part of it had not changed in a very long time.

The streets were nearly deserted as he walked, a city of millions reduced to occasional skittering shadows and receding footsteps. Todtman knew why, of course, but the reminders were still jarring. A man stood on a street corner shouting nonsense and throwing his fists at empty air: shadowboxing. Todtman gave him a wide berth only to walk into a much closer encounter.

"No place for an old man," the stranger spat in Arabic, sizing up Todtman's crisp black suit and loose pale skin. "An old . . . American!"

"Ah," said Todtman, adopting a cordial tone and responding in Arabic, "but old Germans can be found anywhere."

"Do you think that's better?" said the man. He took a step out of the shadows. Many of the city's streetlights were dark now, burned out or broken, but the one above them still flickered grudgingly. As the man stepped farther into its glow, Todtman saw a kitchen knife in his hand.

Todtman gave the man a last, weary smile. He had tried. The blade flashed out fast — but not fast enough. The man was already spinning up and away, tossed through the air like a Frisbee. He hit the pole of the streetlight, and his troubled night came to an oblivious end as he slid limply down to the sidewalk. Todtman continued on.

Outside the café, a man stood guard. Todtman needed no supernatural assistance to know whom the man worked for. He approached him directly. The man's eyes grew round with surprise. The guard reached for something inside his light linen jacket.

"No," Todtman said, and the man stopped. "I will not go inside this place. I will not jeopardize your duties as a guard. It is you, in fact, that I want to talk to."

The man nodded, his hand dropping to his side and his eyes glazing over. The man could not see the amulet Todtman was holding, but he could certainly feel its effects. The Watcher was a complicated symbol. It meant different things in different contexts, but right now it meant *overseer*. Right now, it meant *boss*. And a man like this — a hired hand, used to taking orders — was well within its powers.

"I am looking for a place," said Todtman. "A place you know well . . ."

Todtman posed his question and got his answer. As he turned the corner, the man's eyes cleared. The guard scanned the sidewalk for intruders, then leaned back against the building. For some reason, he felt like he was forgetting something.

A cab sped down the side street and Todtman waved his cane at it. The cabbie had no intention of stopping, but he caught the man's eyes as he passed and found himself pulling over anyway. He was glad he had when he heard the destination: a nearly deserted stretch in the warehouse district near the edge of the city. It meant a hefty fare and fewer crazies. He thought it would be safer. And it would be — if he drove away fast enough. If he escaped the whispering evil that hung over that area like a low, dark cloud.

∩I
∩

Into the Valley

The valley walls were steep and treacherous in the dark. Alex wished they could take the secret path they'd discovered, but it was at least half a mile away and their pursuers were too close to risk it.

He took another step, and the heel of his boot sheared off a chunk of limestone, sending him sliding several feet down the slope on his backside.

"Careful!" hissed Ren.

Alex tried to concentrate on his footing, but he was hounded by questions. *How did The Order find us?* They could have been spotted in town or given away by the cabbie, he supposed. But the pincer move was precise. *In a valley rimmed with slopes and ridges, how did they know exactly which one?*

Distracted, he nearly missed another step. He forced his feverish mind to concentrate on the tricky descent, sliding down the steepest parts on his backside. A crescent moon was just edging into view as they reached the bottom. As

Alex looked back toward it, he saw a host of vague shadows surmount the top of the ridge. Their hunters would indeed follow them here.

Luke clicked on his flashlight and pointed it straight ahead.

"Shut it off," hissed Alex, pointing up the slope. "They're coming."

"How are we supposed to find a hiding place?" Ren whispered urgently. "I can't see anything!"

Alex looked around. He wished he knew what to do, where to go. He wished Todtman was there to tell them. As soon as he thought of the old German, his words came back to him: *"From now on, it is winner take all."*

If The Order got the Spells first, it was all over. And now their forces were in the valley that might hold them. This wasn't a game of hide-and-seek — it was a race! Alex's hand closed around the scarab. "I know a place," he said softly.

And it was true. Even at this distance, Tut's tomb flickered on the edge of his senses. He didn't know if it was the Lost Spells sending such a strong signal, but he knew he needed to find out. "Follow me," he said, and with no other options, the others did.

Alex could feel the ground giving up the day's heat through the soles of his boots as they hurried across the valley floor, but the air had already cooled considerably. The powerful signal from his amulet led him directly across the dark valley, like a plane navigating by radar.

They paused to catch their breath at the entrance to KV 62.

"Wait, here?" said Ren, scanning the dark valley behind them for any signs of their pursuers.

"Yeah," said Alex. "I think the Lost Spells could be in here. Something is. And remember what Todtman —"

But Ren wasn't having it. "Yeah, something is here: bones! And probably a Death Walker."

"He wasn't here last time," said Alex.

"Neither were *the Spells*!"

It was such a crushing comeback that Alex could only respond with open-mouthed silence.

"Ouch," said Luke.

Alex ignored him and tried to regroup. "We didn't have time to really look," he said, before quickly changing tactics. "And we don't have time to argue. If we're caught out in the open now, we're sunk."

"Then we'd better find someplace else quick," said Ren.

Luke looked at both of them and shook his head. "Let's just go in," he said, breaking the standoff. "We don't have time to find someplace else to hide."

Alex made a quick concession to seal the deal: "Any sign of the Walker — even one warm chicken bone — and we're out of here. I promise."

"Fine," huffed Ren. She turned toward Luke: "But you're being dumb." She turned toward Alex: "And I won that debate."

Alex didn't deny it. He'd lost the argument but won the battle. As they filed inside, their backs tensed against the possibility of an Order bullet, he felt a strong urge to pull out his flashlight. He wanted one more look at the symbol they'd spotted the day before. The Aten: the symbol of the sun cult that had been wiped away by Tut's royal decree. It shouldn't have been there, and the fact was nagging at him — one more thing he was sure was trying to tell him something. But he couldn't risk the light giving them away.

They passed the open gate and entered the dark mouth of the tomb. Alex could finally reach into his pack for his flashlight, feeling the reassuring thunk of the Book of the Dead as he did.

They washed the walls thoroughly with their flashlight beams, but the first few rooms looked the same as before. There was one difference, though. Buried beneath the desert, the tomb had been almost pleasantly cool on their first visit. Now it was hot. And the farther in they went, the hotter it got. "Uh, guys?" said Alex.

"Yeah," confirmed Luke. "It's like a brillion degrees in here."

That was enough for Ren. "Any sign, you said. One chicken bone, you said."

Alex protested: "Maybe it just heats up during the day and takes a while —"

"Alex!" said Ren. "Chicken bone!"

Alex dropped his head. She was right: He had promised.

But by the time they got back to the entrance, the choice had been taken from them. Flashlights lit the valley floor outside, the closest no more than twenty yards from the gate and getting closer.

The friends could do nothing but slink back inside before they were spotted, risking an unseen evil to avoid an undeniable danger.

"Let's hide in the treasury room," said Alex. "In the back."

They fled back inside, turned the last few corners, stepped over the piled bones — and the plan came apart.

The treasury would make a lousy hiding place, after all.

It was glowing.

"Let's hide in the treasury room," said Luke, his voice a squeaky, unkind imitation of Alex's.

"We should *not* go in there," added Ren, but Alex already had.

Ren ducked her head in after him. On the back wall of the tomb there was a thin line of yellow light. She moved closer. There was another chamber behind the wall, a lit chamber.

Ren stared at the glowing line and realized that it was slowly shrinking, getting narrower as she watched. Alex darted past her and ran his fingers along the edge of the glowing stone. "A secret room," he said eagerly. "What if this is the hiding place of the Lost Spells?" His voice trailed off as he dug his fingers into the narrowing gap in the wall.

The wall began to slide open. As the gap widened, Ren realized it was a doorway of some sort, but there were no edges, no tracks or hinges. The glowing gap simply expanded — seamlessly, liquidly — as if the stone itself was yawning open.

A wave of heat and light hit Ren as the door opened, and she covered her face with her hands. When she lowered them, she saw neither the burned and blistered face of the Death Walker nor the glowing chamber she had expected.

"Of course," she said, and she really should have known by now. "Of course it's another tunnel."

Tunnel Vision

Alex took a step inside and then hesitated, his hand still on the strange doorway. This wasn't a hiding place for him; it was a path forward. Whatever he'd been sensing in this tomb, it was stronger in here, coming from inside this secret section. He knew it was dangerous, but he was drawn to it. *Could this really be where his mom hid the Spells?* "You two don't have to come," he said. "But I feel like everything is trying to tell me something, and this time I need to listen."

"Alex," said Ren, and he was afraid she was going to say "chicken bone" again. Instead, she said: "Shut it. We're coming."

Alex felt a little swell of emotion. His best friend might argue with him sometimes, but she had never once abandoned him. "Thanks," he whispered, before Luke ruined the moment.

"Move it, guys," he said, brushing past. "The faster we get inside this weird door, the quicker we can shut it behind us."

Neither of them argued with that. For all they knew, The Order was already entering Tut's tomb. The three friends turned and pushed and prodded the edgeless doorway closed. It made a small, dry hiss as stone met stone, leaving them staring at a blank wall. It was a careful-what-you-wish-for moment.

"Uh," said Luke. "Guys? What if that doesn't open again?"

Alex closed his hand around the amulet and tried to sense the workings of the wall in the same way he sensed the inner movements of the locks he picked with the scarab. "I should be able to open this," he said.

Ren exhaled. The three turned back toward the tunnel. It was lit by an intense, unnatural light that seemed to come from everywhere at once. The tunnel sloped downward and curved slightly, hiding what was at the end. And it was hot. Really hot.

"There's definitely something down here," said Alex, still holding his amulet. "This feels . . . bigger than anything we've experienced before." Alex hoped his suspicion was right. "We'll be quiet," he whispered. "Spy mode." It was a game he and Ren had played back at the Met, back when they were just kids who played at adventure.

Ren nodded. "And if you're wrong — if it's the Death Walker's tomb?"

"Then it will tell us who he is — we can figure out the right spell to use and —"

"Not if we're deep-fried first," Luke cut in.

And so they crept forward — carefully — and the deeper they went, the hotter it got.

"Look at the walls," said Ren, reaching up to wipe sweat from her forehead.

Alex was already looking. Intricate hieroglyphic writing covered nearly every inch of the walls near the entrance. Some of the symbols were painted on and some were cut deep into the stone. He wrapped his hand around the scarab, and once again his mind lit up with a single, nearly overwhelming signal. He forced himself to concentrate on the symbols on the wall, and the meanings revealed themselves. The same few words echoed over and over again within the texts: *concealed*, *hidden*, *secret*, *cloaked*, *guarded*.

"What does it mean?" whispered Ren.

Alex could see her hand wrapped around her ibis, her eyes scanning the walls. She was reading the same things he was.

"I think they're spells," he said. "Prayers. Just like in the Book of the Dead."

"But for what?"

Alex looked again, saw the same words take the starring role. The prayers in the Book of the Dead were to help the spirit cross safely over into the afterlife. Words like *protect*, *safe*, and *spirit* were everywhere. But these . . . "I think they're supposed to hide something," he said. A surge of relief and excitement went through him: *It really was a hiding place!* He looked closer at the faded paint and added, "But they're ancient, thousands of years old."

"So the Walker didn't make them?"

Alex shook his head and whispered as they rounded a bend in the tunnel. "If he's here, I think he found this place," he said.

"Hey, Sherlock," hissed Luke. "Eyes on the prize, huh?"

"Right," said Alex. "Sorry." They were deeper now, with an unknowable danger ahead. They stopped talking and crept carefully forward. Forward and down.

The hieroglyphs grew sparser the deeper they went, and the heat increased. Alex's excitement mixed with fear. A fat drop of sweat rolled down his forehead and into one wide-open eye. He wiped the salty sting away with the back of his hand. The hieroglyphs spoke of hiding, but this heat meant danger.

For just a second, he thought he heard a smooth sliding sound coming from behind them, but then they rounded the corner. A large circular chamber lay before them, and the phantom sound was forgotten.

"What the what?" said Luke.

Alex stared at the chamber. He knew exactly what it was. "It's a temple," he whispered. "At least . . . it is now."

The walls of this chamber bore no ancient peeling hieroglyphs. Instead, the broad limestone walls were covered in new ones. And these writings had a recurring theme as well: the Aten.

The sun disk — the symbol of the pure light religion imposed by Tut's father, Akhenaten — was everywhere. All along the wall, royal figures stood staring up at the sky as lines of light and life descended toward them from a massive sun disk on the ceiling. The lines ended in ankhs, held to the figures' mouths and noses like the breath of life.

And in the bright light of the chamber there could be no more doubt about how the symbols were made — or by whom. All the images were black, standing out starkly against the light sandstone walls. Alex stepped forward and carefully touched one of the lines. Dark flakes brushed free on his finger. "Burned," he said. "Burned into the stone."

His heart pounded as he looked around. Fear made the walls feel like they were closing in on him. *Calm down*, he told himself. *This is the Walker's tomb, but the Walker isn't here . . . Focus on the room.* The first thing he saw was the false door — a pair of raised columns framing a painted indentation in the wall — the same ceremonial gateway to the afterlife they'd found in all the other tombs. But he saw none of the treasure and stolen finery they'd found in those other chambers. The room was sparsely decorated and dominated by a low sandstone table in the center. A single ancient clay jar rested atop it. The heat in the chamber was so intense that it stung Alex's lungs as he drew the breath for his next words: "It's an altar."

He'd seen enough. He knew now, beyond a shadow of a doubt in the shadowless room. "The Death Walker is the priest," he said. "From the museum."

Alex heard Ren unzip her pack. He turned and saw her riffling through her notebook. "Akhenotra," she read, "royal priest in the court of pharaoh Akhenaten, died circa 1319 BC."

"That's him," he said. "It has to be. This whole thing is a chapel, a priest's chapel. The Aten is the symbol of Akhenaten's sun cult."

"Okay, great," said Luke. "But we're going to burst into flames. Let's hide in the tunnel until The Order goes away."

Alex knew they couldn't stand this heat much longer, but his eyes continued to scan the room. He still hadn't found what he was looking for. Then he saw it. The little alcove didn't look like much, just a scooped-out hole in the wall with a little shelf inside. The only reason he even looked twice was the hieroglyphs. Small and finely carved, they surrounded the little hole in the wall. He didn't even need to grasp his amulet to recognize the now familiar symbols: *conceal, cloak, hide* . . .

He was sure now. This whole thing: the edgeless doorway, the tunnel, the ancient chamber, the alcove. It wasn't built as a tomb or even as a chapel. It was built to hide one thing.

The Lost Spells.

He turned toward Ren. She'd followed his gaze, and he watched her eyes size up the shelf and light up as she made the same connection. This is where the signal was coming from. It wasn't from where the Spells were but from where they had been. *Like a radioactive trace*, thought Alex in open awe. *Just how powerful are these things?*

"Guys?" said Luke from near the tunnel entrance. "Why aren't we moving yet?"

His mom had been here, in Tut's tomb and in this chamber, he thought. *This is where she'd found the Spells.* And now he was pretty sure he knew why she hadn't put them back: *She'd come back only to find that the hiding place had been discovered.*

But the friends had pushed their luck too far. And now they had been discovered, too.

Words echoed through the chamber. Luke put his hands up in front of him and began backing slowly away from the tunnel.

Alex reached up for his amulet. He needed to: The words coming from the tunnel were in ancient Egyptian.

"He's here," gasped Ren.

Alex barely heard her over the sound of his pulse pounding in his ears. But he saw the first sandaled foot step into the chamber clearly enough, and he saw the second one bring the Walker with it. The old priest turned to regard them — and smiled. A blister on the cheek of his heat-ravaged face burst and the pus ran down his chin, but still he smiled.

"Little blasphemers," he said. "Delivered unto me."

Moths to a Flame

Akhenotra waved his hand and the tunnel entrance sealed behind him, the stone on one side seeming to reach out and fuse with the stone on the other.

Alex's mind flashed to the thin slice of light that had drawn them there in the first place. "You left it open, didn't you?" he said. "To lure us here."

Akhenotra answered vaguely. "Even the most fragile creatures feel safe in the light of the day."

It was a priest's analogy, soothing language for a florid sermon, but Alex was thinking of another saying: *like moths to a flame.*

"*Shouldn't* they feel safe in the sun?" said Alex, trying to keep the Walker talking as he swung the pack off his back with his free hand. The weight shifted within as the pack settled on the floor: the metal clank of the flashlights, the wooden thunk of the Book. "Doesn't the sun give life?"

The Walker huffed out a little laugh, the meaning of which hadn't changed at all in the last three millennia: *nice try.*

"The light was meant for another," he said, his gaze

turning from Alex to Luke and Ren. They were standing near the stone altar in the center of the room, the only meager shelter the chamber provided. "But you three will do for now. I will need my strength for the battle to come."

Akhenotra turned back to Alex and raised his hands above his head. Even as Alex's left hand tightened around his amulet and he felt the electric rush of its power, his right hand tugged on the zipper of his backpack. If it was a battle he wanted . . .

"Your tomb sucks!" called Ren, her small frame nearly eclipsed behind the stone altar.

Akhenotra lowered his hands slightly and turned to face her. "I have modest needs, little one."

"Yeah," she said, the ibis channeling her living words into a long-dead tongue. "Or The Order just doesn't like you! You should see the tombs they built for the others."

Alex knew what she was doing: provoking, distracting. It was a dangerous game. His pack gaped open, revealing a corner of the Book of the Dead.

"I didn't need their help," said Akhenotra. The defensiveness in his voice told Alex that, though his tomb was more modest, vanity was a weakness for this Walker, too. "This chamber was provided for me by the beneficence of the Aten."

"You just found it!" said Alex. Two could play Ren's game. "They wouldn't even build you one."

Akhenotra's broad chest puffed out slightly. "We will work together in the Final Kingdom, when I will rule this land in the name of the Aten."

The Final Kingdom? Alex wanted to know what he meant, but survival mattered more.

"For now, all I need is a place to worship," continued Akhenotra. "And sustenance." He raised his hands again, and this time flames began to form in the air between them. "Enough talk," he said, over the low crackle. "Make peace with your profane gods."

"DON'T LOOK AT IT!"

This time, Ren's warning had come in time.

Alex tore his eyes away from the rolling fire. He yanked out the twin boards holding the ancient texts. Holding his amulet, his eyes washed across the small, precise hieroglyphs. He knew who the Walker was now, so he was pretty sure he could figure out the right spell. Something about the sun, maybe, or priests, or . . .

"Look out, Alex!" cried Ren.

Alex swung his head back around and flame filled his vision. The Walker had released his fireball, and it was rocketing toward him.

Instinctively, disastrously, Alex raised his hands, which still held the ancient text. The Book of the Dead became a shield for the living, as the flaming sphere crashed into the tightly held boards. Dry wood and ancient papyrus that had survived thousands of years instantly went up in smoke, and Alex was left shaking his burned fingers.

"Nooo!" cried Ren.

Alex's heart dropped, but he wrapped his heat-stung hand around his scarab.

"That is twice you have surprised me, little heretic," said Akhenotra. "There won't be a third time."

Alex felt the heat of the chamber against his sweat-slick skin. His right hand was at his side, like a gunfighter's, as he waited for Akhenotra to make his next move. *He'll raise his arms over his head and look up*, he thought. *That's how he summons the fire; that's why his face is so scarred.*

But what was Alex's next move? The Book was gone, along with any hope of banishing the Walker. Escape was their only option — but where could they run if The Order was still right outside? Alex felt cornered, desperate.

Luke was just looking for a way out. He'd used his speed to sprint around behind the Walker and was pawing uselessly at the spot where the tunnel entrance had been, but the bare wall offered no handle to pull, no knob to turn.

Alex was sure he could open it. Maybe if they made it back to the tomb above, they could seal the Walker inside . . . A plan formed: He'd wait for the Walker to raise his hands, hit him with a concentrated spear of wind, and then they'd run.

Instead, Akhenotra's jaw suddenly dropped open. Flame poured from his open mouth. Alex lurched to the side and tried to fall back out of the way —

"AAAAAAH!" he screamed as he felt the searing flames burn through his shirt and bite into the soft flesh of his left shoulder.

"Alex!" shouted Ren.

He had fallen to the ground. He rolled onto his side and

grabbed the wound with his right hand. His skin felt scalding hot and alarmingly wet.

His eyes blurred with tears but he forced himself to look up. Ren had one hand on the stone altar and one hand stretched out toward him, as if trying to pull him safely toward home base in some childhood game. Luke was pounding both fists against solid stone.

Akhenotra walked calmly toward Alex, looming over him. He was speaking, but Alex had dropped his amulet and couldn't understand him. The temperature in the chamber had soared, and Alex felt on the verge of passing out from the heat and pain.

The Death Walker raised his hands, and fresh flames began to form. Alex allowed himself to look at them this time. For a few merciful moments the hypnotic trance eased the burning in his shoulder, eased the knowledge of the world of pain to come and the oblivion to follow.

He had come halfway across the world: searching for his mom, chasing ghosts, and now it would all end here.

But . . . There was a noise: a smooth sliding sound from along the wall.

But . . . The Walker turned toward it, the flames above him flickering.

But . . . *What is it?* Alex didn't understand what was going on, or why he was still alive. And then he raised his head enough to see the passageway opening again and Luke stepping aside to make way.

Tut.

Royal Rumble

The boy king, Tutankhamun, glided gracefully into the chamber. His crimson robes flowed vividly in the bright light.

Akhenotra glared at him with a look that held both anger and awe.

Though Alex's right hand still held the warm slick mess of his wounded left shoulder, he slowly raised his left toward his amulet. It hurt tremendously, but this exchange would determine whether he and his friends lived or died. The friends who had followed him into mortal danger.

"Hello, priest," said Tut. "Hello, traitor."

"You are the traitor!" spat Akhenotra.

"Well," said Tut, making a casual circle with one hand. "I was just thinking that since you killed your pharaoh and all . . ."

Akhenotra smiled wickedly, and then his image shifted again, just as it had in the desert. There was a brief veil of heat haze, and when it subsided, an old man in ornate ancient garb stood in his place. "It was easy, you know?" said Akhenotra, the priest's voice coming from the old man's lips. "Who would stop your humble cupbearer, your most trusted servant, from entering your chamber as you slept?"

"Mmmm," said Tut, unimpressed and slowly advancing on his enemy. "A trick of the light, a cheap charade . . . It is still treason to kill your pharaoh."

"You were never my pharaoh," said Akhenotra, the false image fading away and his old form returning. "You are the snake who undid your father's good work."

"Who abolished his silly cult, you mean?" said Tut, advancing farther, the tunnel door already beginning to slide shut behind him. "The Aten was a gimmick. What is the sun without the rain, the day without the night?"

Akhenotra unleashed a roar of anger at Tut's words, and before the scream stopped, the flames began. A blazing orange and red stream poured from the priest's mouth toward Tut. Alex watched in horror, Ren gophered her head back beneath the altar, and Luke, who'd been tiptoeing toward the fading doorway behind Tut, dove for cover.

But Tut merely pressed both hands together in front of him as if praying. The flames broke on his hands like a wave splitting against a pier. Tut was shrouded in fire.

Finally, Akhenotra snapped his mouth shut.

And there was Tut. Here and there, patches of his robes had turned black, and a few spots smoldered. But Tut's face remained calm. "You have misused my royal robes," he said, looking down at one sleeve. As he did, he caught Alex's eyes. "And my strange friends."

"And you destroyed the religion I gave my *life* to!" roared Akhenotra, taking a step toward Tut and holding one hand up in front of him. Heat haze shimmered in his palm, and when it faded, the priest held a fierce-looking ceremonial mace. Its copper head was heavy and ringed with spikes, and Alex had the sinking feeling that this image was no illusion.

In response, Tut waved one arm toward the floor. The sleeve of his robe snapped from the quick, crisp movement, and suddenly Tut held a vicious, sickle-bladed sword. Alex stared at it as he struggled to sit up. It was a *khopesh*, Tut's royal sword.

Tut raised the blade and rushed toward Akhenotra, who raised his mace and closed the last few steps between them. The weapons came together with a loud clang.

It. Was. On.

Alex released his amulet and tried to push himself to his feet. He made it halfway before gasping with pain and beginning to fall back. A small hand stopped his fall, grabbing his right forearm. Ren. And then a strong arm slid under his back from the other side. Luke. Together, they raised him to his feet.

"Are you okay?" said Ren, eyeing his red-and-oozy wound with concern.

"It really hurts," he admitted. "But I think it's just on the surface."

"There's not much surface left there, bro," said Luke.

PORRanngg!

KLANG!

The weapons continued to clash in the center of the chamber.

"We have to help Tut!" said Ren, shifting her gaze from Alex's shoulder to his eyes.

"We have to get out of here!" said Luke.

Ren was right. "First Tut," Alex said. "If he can take out Akhenotra, we're safe from The Order in here." But Alex had no idea what to do. He reached for his amulet again, so that he could at least know what Tut was saying.

"Where is it?" Tut shouted, bringing his sword down hard only to have it blocked by the thick handle of the mace. He brought his sword up and down four more times in quick succession, each blow blocked but each accompanied by a word.

"Where . . ." *Klong!*

"Is . . ." *Plonk!*

"My . . ." *Pring!*

"Heart!" *Swanhkk!*

Akhenotra spun away deftly and delivered a sweeping blow of his own. "I took it with me," he said as Tut stepped back and the mace head ripped at the front of his robes. "A peace offering to the god you betrayed."

"His heart," whispered Alex, his head reeling as old, familiar facts clicked into place. The Ancient Egyptians always left the heart in the body during mummification; Tut was the only pharaoh ever discovered without one. "Akhenotra took his heart."

Without the heart, Tut couldn't go through the weighing of the heart ceremony to gain entrance into the afterlife. He would be forever between worlds. Alex looked at the boy king, betrayed in both life and death. Now he understood what Tut had been searching for out in the desert — and the force behind those blows.

"He must be so mad," said Ren.

As if in answer, Tut brought the sword down one more time. "Where is it?" he shouted.

"It is my greatest offering," said Akhenotra, raising his mace to block the blow. "And I will —"

The force of the swing was too great. The heavy curved blade of Tut's *khopesh* cut clean through the handle of the mace and sunk deep into the Death Walker's chest. Both halves of the mace thunked to the floor.

Akhenotra finished his sentence with a weak, distracted voice: ". . . offer it up along with you."

For a few moments, the two combatants just stood there looking at the spot where the blade had sunk in. Then Akhenotra stumbled backward. Tut released the sword, and it went with him.

"Yes!" said Ren.

But the Death Walker didn't fall.

"Why are you still standing?" said Tut.

Akhenotra finally pulled his eyes away from his wound

and looked up. "You can't kill me," he said, his tone more of realization than defiance. "I am already dead."

Alex dropped his head. The pain in his shoulder, the heat in the room, the hopelessness of the situation . . . It all washed over him at once, swamping his defenses. His knees felt wobbly. "The Book of the Dead," he mumbled, glancing over at the pile of ash and charred wood on the floor. "I can't believe I got it fried."

"Yes," said the priest. "You made that so easy for me." Then he reached out and wrapped his hand around the hilt of the sword and slowly — and with a deeply disgusting sound — pulled it free of his own chest. He smiled triumphantly. "I am invincible," he crowed, admiring his new weapon.

But when he looked up, Tut was smiling, too. "I hope this isn't indelicate of me," he said. "But if it's the Book of the Dead we need . . ."

He raised his hands to his neck and peeled his burned and torn robes to the side. ". . . then there's something you should know," he continued.

His robes fell to the ground with a soft thud. The body beneath was covered in linen, and the linen was covered in rows of precise hieroglyphic writing and tiny, colorful paintings. "I am wrapped in it."

Have a Heart

Ren stared at the tiny symbols covering Tut's tightly wrapped frame. She'd seen the Book of the Dead printed on mummy wrappings before, but those had been covering dried-out husks in glass cases or on scraps of linen that had been flattened out and framed — not wrapped around moving legs and muscular shoulders. But there was a problem. A big one: "We still don't know what spell," she said.

"You have to use the ibis!" Alex said.

Ren scanned the room: the brilliant, unnatural sunlight; the heat so intense she felt like she was being microwaved; Tut unarmed and dressed only in bandages; Luke near the door in a wide sports stance but with nowhere to run; Alex badly injured; and the Death Walker stepping forward.

Akhenotra's first step was hesitant and unsure. The sword strike had taken something out of him. But by his second step he was already recovering.

Ren's first move was hesitant and unsure, too. She reached slowly for the ibis, dreading the flood of images. It had both helped them and hurt them. She still remembered stepping

164

forward and confidently waving the Walker over in the desert. How was she supposed to know that image had been a
warning? It's not like the thing had an answer key.

Akhenotra advanced on Tut, who took a step back.

She had no choice. She closed her hand around the ibis
and felt the warm, white stone against her palm.

Ren had never been as smart as she'd wanted to be — not
as brilliant as her dad or as effortlessly gifted as her brightest
classmates — but she'd always closed the gap with effort.
She did the extra work to prepare and attacked the extra
credit. She always crushed those questions, because they
could only help and not hurt, so she could relax.

There'd be no relaxing now. This test could hurt; this test
could kill. She held her breath, closed her eyes, and tried her
absolute hardest to grab each image as it passed.

A stone ram, eyes open, curled horns forward . . .

A simple but elegant boat, two painted oars at the back . . .

A gold and blue falcon, at rest, as if nesting . . .

A circle of fire . . .

Her eyes snapped open — she'd seen too much fire
already. The amulet fell from her hand. "What am I looking
for?" said Alex. "Something to do with fire, maybe?"

She blinked over at him, refocusing her eyes. He'd taken
a few steps toward Tut and was already scanning the wrappings. "I . . ." she began. "I'm not . . ."

*Why couldn't the amulet just show me Tut's stomach or armpit
or wherever the right spell was?* she thought. *What did a boat
have to do with it?*

"Hurry!" said Alex.

Akhenotra took another step forward, much surer on his feet now, and raised the sword.

Ren saw Alex wince as he grasped his amulet and pointed his hand at the approaching enemy. Wind shot forth and knocked Akhenotra back a few steps.

Alex tried another blast, but this time the Walker leaned into it. Alex was weakening, and she watched in horror as the wind died down and the blade of the sword suddenly burst into flame. The sun priest slashed the air with the fiery blade, admiring his work. He had made the weapon his own.

She parsed the images again. *A ram? A falcon? A boat? Fire? Were these clues*, she wondered, *or warnings? Was the answer in there . . . somewhere?*

"Which spell?" called Alex.

"There's a ram and a bird — a falcon, I think," she called, "a boat, some fire . . ."

"Which one?" shouted Alex. "What exactly am I looking for?"

Her pulse pounding in her ears, her head full of too much information and too little context, she finally called out the horrible truth: "I don't know!"

Alex stared at Ren in disbelief. It seemed so strange to see a straight-A student straight up fail, but there was no denying it: Plus Ten Ren was minus ten in magic.

If they were going to live, it was up to him. He quickly scanned Tut's wrappings. *Falcon*, she'd said, but that was useless. The falcon symbol was part of half a dozen common hieroglyphs — there was a flock of them scattered over Tut's wrappings. What was the other thing, a ram?

Before Alex could get a good look, Tut backed up quickly and nearly shoulder checked him. Alex wasn't used to his books moving. He ducked his head around the undead monarch and saw the Death Walker raise his flaming sword for another chop. The first one had missed, but . . .

"We need to buy some time!" Alex shouted to his friends.

"With what?" said Luke. "There's nothing in here."

But that wasn't exactly true.

"I got your jar, Mister Blister!" called Ren.

She had circled around the fighting and was once again standing behind the stone altar in the center of the chamber. This time she was holding up the single, ancient jar that had rested atop it. It was one of the few artifacts in the room and located in a position of honor. Alex figured it was worth a shot — but he didn't expect it to provoke such a strong reaction.

Akhenotra whirled around, the curved sword still raised above his head in wood-chopping position. "Put that down, girl!" he shouted, extending the sword toward her menacingly as he began striding toward the altar. "That is for the Aten!"

Ren's eyes grew huge, and Alex knew she hadn't expected quite so strong a reaction, either. "Uh," she said.

"End around!" shouted Luke. With his sprinter's speed,

he crossed the chamber in no time flat and cut behind Ren with his hands out.

Ren had seen enough football games to know what to do. She turned and executed a perfect handoff into Luke's gut. Luke took the jar and sped toward the far side of the chamber. The Death Walker followed, breaking into a run of his own. Whatever was in that jar was important, but Alex had no time to wonder why that was.

He got to work. Ram, falcon, boat, fire: He saw all of those things, as hieroglyphs or in the paintings. Too many choices. He looked for them all in the same spell, but it was hard — Tut wouldn't stop moving. As Akhenotra traced a sandal-slapping circle around the room in pursuit of Luke, Tut turned to watch. He had developed a sudden interest in the jar himself.

"Uh, Tut?" said Alex. No response. "Your, um, majesty?" he ventured. Still nothing. He gave up and started turning along with the text, trying to keep up despite the heat and pain. But then he saw something he hadn't expected among the symbols.

Is that . . . an Aten? he wondered. His brain told him it was, but his amulet told him something else. It was a sun disk, but not the Aten. It was a symbol of Amun-Re, the sun god that reigned before and after the short-lived cult. Amun-Re was "one of the biggies," as his mom liked to say, and Alex knew plenty about him. He knew that Tut had changed his own name from Tut-Ankh-Aten to Tut-Ankh-Amun in the sun god's honor. He also knew that the symbols for Amun-Re included both the falcon and the ram.

He quickly read the title of the prayer: "For sailing in the Great Boat of Amun-Re and passing safely over . . ."

"Uh, your majesty-ness," he said to Tut, tapping one shoulder. "Could you raise your arm?"

"Hmmm?" said Tut. "Oh, certainly."

Tut raised his right arm and Alex read the rest: ". . . the circle of flame."

Fire. *This is it*, thought Alex. *It has to be . . . And Amun-Re will definitely want a word with this dude.*

Alex risked a quick glance up and saw Akhenotra barely a sword-length behind Luke, who was red-faced and gasping in the intense heat. Alex filled his lungs with overheated air and began to recite the words:

"For this is the flame which burns behind Re . . ."

The words hit Akhenotra like a cramp in the side, and his steady stride faltered. Luke pulled away. Akhenotra called out to him, a note of desperation slipping into his voice, "Give me the offering, child."

Luke looked back: "Yeah, right!"

The anger rushed back into the Death Walker's blister-scarred visage: "Give me the heart!" he bellowed.

Tut turned again, and Alex barely managed to keep his place. The boy king uttered an ancient expression that loosely translated to: "Say what, now?"

Alex wanted to plead with him to hold still, but he couldn't break his chant or he'd have to start over. And there'd be no time for that. The Walker had identified the threat now, and was striding straight back toward them. Alex grabbed Tut's shoulder with his free hand, holding him in place, and surrendered himself to the ancient text. "A path is laid for me . . ."

His chant gained strength and a phantom chorus rose up to whisper along. "My protection is that of Re . . ."

As he neared the end, the text shook, nearly jarring him out of his trance. Instead, he gripped Tut's shoulder tighter and sang the next word louder. He was too close now. Another sudden shudder, faint voices screaming at him from another world, but he dared not look away.

He completed the spell. ". . . For I am He who travels, the Greater God."

He blinked his eyes, the color returning to them. He released Tut and stepped back as the world of the living slowly came into focus.

Tut was standing with his own bronze sword buried deep in his chest, the blade no longer aflame but still sizzling slightly. Now Alex understood why the text had shaken so much. And Akhenotra — Alex gazed at the space in front of Tut — Akhenotra wasn't standing at all.

The Death Walker was on his back, his knees and hands pulling up and back above him as his carcass aged hundreds of years with each second, the skin drying and shriveling into the dark, taut leather of a mummy.

Alex stepped around to get a better look at Tut, and the others rushed over to join him. He grasped his amulet once more, despite the pounding headache that using it for so long was beginning to cause him. "Are you okay?" he asked doubtfully, staring at the sword embedded in Tut's chest and a second large gash next to it. Sliced and burned wrappings peeled away from either side.

"I'm not sure," said Tut, his voice soft. He tried to take a small step and his knees buckled slightly. "But it doesn't matter now. Let me see the jar."

Huffing and puffing and gaping openly at the sword-wound, Luke handed it over.

"Thank you," said Tut, the imperious teen surprising them all by bowing slightly. "You have a strange name, Duuuuude, but fast feet."

Luke couldn't understand a word of it, but Ren answered for him. "And you've got . . ." she began. She paused as Tut lifted the ancient lid, and then completed her sentence: ". . . a lot of heart."

A broad smile blossomed on Tut's face as he replaced the lid. He stepped forward, touched Alex lightly on his injured shoulder, and said, "I am sorry for your pain."

To Alex's surprise the touch didn't hurt his scorched shoulder at all. As he looked down, he saw why: The black-edged hole burned into his shirt now framed healthy skin, no tanner — or redder — than usual.

"How —" he began but was cut off by a soft, metallic clang.

He looked up and saw that the sword had fallen to the ground.

There was nothing left to hold it up.

King Tutankhamun was gone.

A moment later, the room went dark.

Dark Deeds

In the pitch-dark of the underground chamber, Luke couldn't remember where he'd dropped his backpack. He knew it had come off when the dead dude was chasing him, but he had no idea where or when. The others were searching for their discarded packs, too, and for a few minutes he just stood there in the dark and let them.

Luke had a lot on his mind, and he was in no huge hurry to leave the chamber. Down here, they were all on the same team, all playing a part. Down here, they were safe. Plus, it was already cooling down.

"I think I found yours, Ren!" Alex called from somewhere near the back wall. "Wait, never mind — it's mine!"

A moment later, Alex's flashlight clicked on. Luke got busy pretending to get busy finding his pack. It was easier now with some light, and pretty soon, they all had their packs on and their flashlights pointed at the section of wall where the door had been.

Luke's fingertips were still raw from desperately clawing the stone for the slightest opening. But then he saw Alex's flashlight click off, and he knew he was getting ready to use his amulet. He was confident his cousin would get them out; he was good with that magic bug. Sure enough, a few moments later, a narrow gap yawned open under the flashlight beams. Luke stepped forward and got a hand on it. He pushed until the strange doorway was open the rest of the way.

"Should we stay here for a while?" he said once they were in the tunnel.

"No," said Ren. "I've been thinking . . ."

Figures, thought Luke.

"We rushed in here like a herd of elephants. If they pick up our trail, they could find this door — or just leave people here. I think we need to get out before we're trapped."

That was good enough for Alex, but Luke had a bad feeling as they headed toward Tut's tomb. Part of that was thirst and exhaustion and peeling skin. But there was something else, something bigger.

He considered the other two as he walked. His flashlight beam danced off Ren's back. She was barely as tall as a batting tee, but she'd come through again. Alex was just ahead of her. Luke glanced up at him. The little dude had straight up been barbecued and still taken care of business. It seemed amazing to him that just a few weeks ago, he'd thought of both of them as little twerps. But then, a lot of the things he'd thought and done over that time seemed unbelievable.

They reached the doorway at the top of the tunnel and

paused while Alex opened it. "It's like picking a lock," he said. "I just have to find the weak point."

Behind him, Luke winced unseen.

There was no light to give them away now, and they switched off their flashlights as the doorway slid open. But the tomb was dark and quiet beyond. They stepped out cautiously, switched their flashlights back on, and pointed them at the floor.

"King Tut's tomb," whispered Ren as the battered and lightly toasted crew shuffled through the famous chambers. When they'd seen it the first time, it had been a bone-strewn archaeological site. Now it felt like walking through a friend's place after he'd moved away.

"That dude was all right," said Luke, almost to himself.

"Funny, he said the same thing about you — Duuuude," said Ren.

Luke let out a little laugh, but he secretly wished she wouldn't be so nice. It made everything harder for him. There was no sign of The Order inside, but they grew quiet again as they neared the exit. The cool night air soothed their skin, and moonlight filled the tunnel mouth as the three crept forward. Before they even made it to the shark-cage gate, they could see the flashlights and hear the muffled words of their pursuers. But they were no longer right in front of the tomb.

"They're heading away," whispered Alex. Luke leaned out and saw the sun-bleached bone of the back of Peshwar's mask glowing eerily in the faint moonlight. They were slowly moving on. It was good news, but Luke's heart sank.

"We should go now, before they change their mind or send someone back," whispered Ren.

Alex agreed: "We can slip off in the other direction if we stay low and move quietly."

The open valley lay in front of them and the murderous hunting party lurked behind. His cousin was right: They probably could make it.

But Luke could never allow that. Not this close. Not when they might see him, too, and know he helped.

His head swam and his guts churned. For a moment, he thought he might throw up, right then and there. He almost wished he would. It would do the job well enough. He couldn't believe he'd gotten himself into this mess.

It had seemed so easy at first. They'd just wanted information. And they'd paid well for it. Well enough that he would be able to get private coaching, the best equipment, everything he'd need to live his dream.

But then they'd gone further — way too far. He'd wanted to quit then. He'd tried to quit. He thought knocking out the guy on the train was a pretty effective resignation. Then he'd made that last phone call in Luxor . . .

He filled his lungs with cool night air.

For a few more steps, that was all he did. But then he forced himself to remember that call, the actual words: *We'll kill them. We'll kill your parents.*

"HEY!" he shouted. "We're over here!"

Alex and Ren swung around, the moonlight delicately tracing the shock on their faces. A moment later, the sound of boots, running hard, filled the air.

"I'm sorry," Luke said, punishing himself by looking his friends in the eyes.

"Luke . . ." said Alex, and the disappointment and hurt in his voice smashed Luke's heart like glass.

"I had to," he said, his own tone just as heavy.

"I can't believe . . ." said Ren, wrestling with it. "*You're* the mole?"

Luke looked down, his friends' expressions already burned into his memory. "I'm sorry," he repeated. Then he stood up tall and pointed down at his crouched comrades.

"OVER HERE!" he shouted again.

A Grave Situation

The worst part for Alex was that he kind of *could* believe it. He'd wanted to believe that his cooler, older cousin really did like him, really was his friend. And maybe he'd wanted that too much, because the memories flashed through his mind now. Every time Luke had slipped away to make a phone call — and every time The Order had been waiting for them. And not just in Egypt. He remembered how Luke had "stalled" the cult's thugs *just* long enough for Alex to arrive at a museum in London. He remembered the sight of Ren knocked out on the floor and the eerie sense that they'd all been waiting for him. It had been a trap . . .

The crack of a rifle and the ping of a bullet jarred him back to brutal reality. Luke took off running, not so much toward the hunters as away from the prey. Alex watched him go, and other memories went with him: of the times he'd helped them, saved them. Could it all have been just to gain their trust? The sky lit up red.

An energy dagger exploded into the sandy ground at Alex's feet with a vicious crackle. For a second he and Ren were lit clearly in the night. A chorus of rifle fire followed, and the two remaining friends dove for cover.

Ren made a small sound, like a yelp, as she hit the ground.

"Are you hit?" Alex gulped.

"I'm okay," she gasped.

The night lit up red again. Another energy dagger zoomed just over Ren's head. Peshwar was getting closer and finding her range. The rifles sounded in the crimson light, but even as the volley of bullets flew one way, Alex sent a wave of wind and sand back the other. Turned toward the enemy with his right hand outstretched, Alex felt a bullet tear through the nylon of his pack. The impact tugged him a few inches back — which is how much the next bullet missed him by.

"Not the boy!" he heard Peshwar shout. "Kill the little one, the girl."

It was Alex's worst nightmare: His best friend paying for his life with hers.

As another dagger came flying through the night, Alex and Ren raced back into the only cover the moonlit valley floor offered: Tut's tomb. Alex slammed the gate behind him with his hand and then spent precious seconds locking it with his amulet. He had no illusions that a shark-cage gate could stop a lioness, but maybe it could buy them enough time.

They rushed back into the pitch-dark tomb to the sound of shouts and boots behind them.

"We're trapping ourselves!" huffed Ren.

"The secret doorway —" said Alex.

"But Luke . . ." Ren said. "Luke knows about it."

"Maybe they won't be able to get it open. It's our best chance."

And now that they were back inside the tomb, it was the only one left.

They raced through the now familiar tomb, the sound of crashing metal behind them speeding their steps as they crossed the treasury chamber.

The strange doorway had already slid halfway closed since their exit, protecting its secret like healing a wound. Ren rushed through the narrow gap and Alex turned his shoulders to follow.

Once inside he glanced back at the shrinking portal. *Hurry, little doorway,* he thought.

"Come on," hissed Ren.

They rushed down the tunnel, their flashlight beams lightning-bugging in front of them. They reached the second doorway and Alex turned sideways and sucked in his chest to squeeze inside.

"Maybe they won't find the entrance," he said, peering out the gap — but a moment later, light leaked into the top of the tunnel. Voices echoed down it, and then footsteps. The first doorway hadn't closed fast enough. The friends watched from the inside as the second doorway finally slid shut, sealing them in the ancient underground chamber.

They both knew this was where they'd make their final stand.

Ren swung her flashlight around, confirming that Akhenotra was still out of commission. She remembered Todtman's warning: Without the Lost Spells, the Walkers might be able to come back again.

She could hear Alex breathing next to her. "What do we do now?" she said.

"We wait, I guess," he whispered back. "I try to keep this door shut: my amulet against her mask."

"And if it doesn't work?"

"Then we fight."

Ren nodded. Easy for him to say. His amulet had some teeth. Hers seemed more confusing than dangerous. Then she remembered something. She swung her flashlight across the floor until the beam reflected back at her. She went over and picked up Tut's sword, still warm to the touch.

"Do you know how to use that thing?" asked Alex as she returned to his side.

"No idea," she admitted.

Two quick thuds cut the conversation short.

"They're hitting the other side," said Alex. "With a rifle or something."

Another thud, and then silence.

"If they get in . . ." Ren began. She shuddered deeply in the still warm chamber as she pictured it. A pack of armed gunmen bursting into the chamber, followed by the lioness . . .

"We don't have much of a chance," said Alex softly, confirming her fears. "If only there were some other way out. Some other . . ."

His flashlight swept along the wall and then stopped. "There! I see a . . ." But his voice trailed off. It was just the false door. The space between the columns was solid rock, painted reddish orange. It was a symbolic gateway for the dead, but a dead end for the living.

Behind them, the wall cracked open and a long gap appeared, lit by electric light. Alex grasped his amulet and tried to push back with his mind against Peshwar's magic. But four strong hands reached into the gap and began to pull. The opening grew.

Alex dropped the amulet. He and Ren rushed behind the altar, the only cover the room had to offer, nearly tripping over the death-curled Death Walker. As the doorway slid open, light spilled into the chamber. They crouched behind the stone slab as an electric lantern lit the room around them. It was a sad game of hide-and-seek: a game they couldn't win for a price they couldn't pay.

Alex leaned closer and whispered: "When they come in, I'll go at them with everything I've got. If I can hold them off for long enough, maybe you can sneak —"

"No!" said Ren, a little too loud. "I am *not* leaving you here."

She felt the weight of the sword in her hand and understood its futility.

As the voices entered the chamber and the lantern reduced their hiding place to a shrinking puddle of shadow, she slowly put down the sword.

As Alex whispered two last words — "Get ready" — her hand moved to her amulet.

Alex's scarab could do so much — had done so much. The ibis had helped them in London but been completely unreliable here, confusing as much as it cleared up. *Why?*

Ren couldn't understand the lioness's words, but she could hear the footsteps getting closer. She knew her best friend would pop up and start fighting soon, and that their last battle would begin and end in this chamber.

What am I doing wrong? she asked herself. *I am trying even harder now. Whenever I use it, I try so hard . . .*

And just like that, she thought she understood. There was only one way to know for sure. As she slowly wrapped her hand around her amulet, she formed a few words of her own. The hunters were too close now even for whispers, so she said them in her head.

She hadn't earned her A's on the tests alone. She put too much pressure on herself and froze up or overthought things sometimes. But the extra credit, whether questions or assignments: That's where she earned her A's. Because there were no wrong answers there. They could only help, never hurt. No pressure, everything free for the taking.

Extra credit, she said to herself. *Anything the ibis gives me is more than we have now.* She didn't squint down and hold her breath. She just closed her eyes and let the images come. To her surprise, there was only one this time. Simple and clear.

"Alex," she said, opening her eyes.

But Alex was already standing up. His hand was around his own amulet, and a sudden powerful wind wiped away her words. He ducked back down next to her and she tried again: "Alex!"

But gunfire and the crackle of an energy dagger drowned out her words. Bullets chipped rock from the back wall, and the crimson energy exploded into the altar in front of them, lighting the chamber like a red dawn.

"Give up now or I will kill you both," called Peshwar in English. "It was never my wish to spare you."

Ren shouted in Alex's ear: "Blast her one more time and then run as hard as you can through that!" She pointed toward the false door along the wall to their right.

As she did, she saw the toe of a boot poke out from the side of the altar. One of the gunmen had reached them. Ren reached down and — in one quick motion, as the bullet slid into the chamber of the rifle above them — she brought the sword up and down.

"AAAAAAAH!" cried the man, blood rushing out the chopped-off end of his boot.

"Never mind," Ren shouted, dropping the sword and grabbing Alex's shoulder. "Go now!"

They sprang to their feet and rushed past the one-and-a-half-footed gunman. Alex swiped his free hand out to the side, releasing a fan of concentrated air to hold their attackers off, but a red glow grew in the room.

As the energy dagger flew straight toward the sprinting friends, Ren rushed toward the painted stone of the false door, dragging Alex behind her.

"What are you doing?" he shouted.

"Trust me!" she called back. It was her turn to take the lead, but she still had doubts. She'd seen herself stepping through this thing, but if she was wrong . . .

"Wait!" called Alex, but his legs kept churning.

She braced for the dull thud of stone, the possibility of impact, as she ran headfirst into the false door. But instead of a crash, she felt a strange, static *POP!*

She had run straight through the wall — and out of the world she knew.

She found herself in a strange twilight realm, lit only by the dim glow of a distant horizon. Her body felt as if it were suspended in some unseen liquid, and there was a loud buzzing in her ears. It was a shadowy dream world, but she could feel it humming all around her like a high-voltage wire, and she knew deep down that it was both real and dangerous.

A moment later, she felt Alex's weight under her hand again as she dragged him through the portal behind her. She dug her hand tight into his arm but didn't dare look back.

All around her, strange sights and sounds vied for her attention. Human voices, human faces, and other voices, too, other shapes. She saw a stronger light in front of her, a glowing square. She ran toward it, her feet feeling slow and heavy. She pulled Alex along, terrified she would lose her grip.

She tried to shout out to him, but there was no oxygen in her lungs, and none around them. And yet she felt fine, as if she'd never needed air in the first place.

A massive serpent cut across her vision, as long as two city buses — an image out of a nightmare. Her eyes grew wide. She ran faster, pulled harder. The square of light was just ahead, revealing itself for what it really was. Could she reach it before the ghostly serpent reached them?

Its mouth was opening now, an abyss of blackness behind long, gray fangs. Another step, another tug, and the light of the doorway swallowed them. The serpent vanished into memory.

Dark again.

"Alex?" she said, surprised to find air in her lungs.

Silence, and then . . .

"Mmmm. Air conditioning."

Ren put her hand down and felt cool tile. They were lying on the floor. The air around them crisp, almost cold . . .

She rose to one knee and her eyes slowly adjusted to the weak light. There were tall windows along the wall, framing an unfamiliar nighttime scene. And inside, a soft electric glow that Ren had known her entire life.

"It's a museum," she said. "We're in a museum."

She didn't know which museum, or where, but she knew what wing they were in. The ancient Egyptian false door behind them told her that much.

Epilogue

Truth and Consequences

Head still reeling, Alex took a moment to assess his surroundings. The museum setting calmed his frayed nerves slightly as he leaned forward to read a small silver-gray information plaque. He knew the language well enough. His father was Egyptian, but his mother's family . . . "It's German," he whispered.

"Are we in *Germany*?" said Ren.

"I don't know," said Alex. His head was swimming with too many questions to list, much less answer. He gazed out a tall window at the placid night beyond, where sleek, modern streetlights glowed softly. "Maybe," he added.

"How is that possible?" said Ren.

He shook his head. He felt like a small boat bobbing up and down on waves of disbelief. "No idea."

But Ren kept at it. "Did we just travel through . . ."

"I think so," Alex said, admitting it as much to himself as to her. "We just traveled through the afterlife."

A look of horror dawned on Ren's face, and she looked down at her own hand as if expecting to find a skeleton there. "It's okay," said Alex. "I think the false doors, and the amulets — *your* amulet . . ." He smiled at her.

But as he took a step toward her, his foot broke an invisible beam, and the museum's state-of-the-art laser security system lit up the room with a fireworks show of flashing light and blaring noise.

They didn't know what they were doing — or where they were going — but they'd had plenty of experience running at this point. They followed the glowing arrows of the exit signs as the sounds of shouts and footsteps joined the cacophony.

Ren spotted the front doors first and arrived a few seconds ahead of Alex. He looked back over his shoulder and saw a pair of guards rushing down a grand marble staircase. He turned back to the doors and reached for his amulet to try to unlock them.

But Ren was already holding her amulet. Before he could even take hold of his, he saw a white glow flash from her closed fist and heard a loud *click!*

"Got it!" she said.

Alex looked over at her, a strange mix of surprise and pride washing through him. "That's new," he managed.

"Just push!" she said.

The friends shouldered through the door and bolted like racehorses into the night. Alex felt both freedom and frustration, triumph and sorrow. They'd failed to recover the Lost Spells and lost a friend, but they'd banished a Death Walker. He'd picked up his mom's trail but was left with nothing more than a name from the past. Angela Felini had taken care of him — and moved away. *Was this his mom's way of saying that she was moving on, too?* It was a terrifying thought, but he had no way to know for sure.

What he did know: There was still work to do, and the time for babysitters was over. *Was he on his own, then?* He looked over at the boot-chopping, amulet-wielding best friend running beside him. *Far from it.*

$$\longleftarrow\!\!+\!\!-\!\!+\!\!-\!\!+\!\!\longrightarrow$$

Luke's arm was bent uncomfortably behind his back, held there by one of The Order's thugs. Peshwar stood in front of him outside the tomb.

"Listen, Peshwawa, or whatever — I did what you wanted," he said.

"You have failed us," she said in her harsh, sandpaper voice. "Again."

"What?" he said. "I . . . I mean, sure, I had to do a few things to 'gain their trust' — just like you said — but I still . . . I mean, that dude on the train was unconscious when I got there."

"I am not talking about that, though of course you are lying," she said, her English just as proficient, and emotionless, as her Arabic. "Your shout was badly timed. It gave them time to get back into the tomb and escape . . . for now."

"Hey," said Luke. "My job was to give you information — or give you Alex. I tried. It's not my fault if you dropped the ball."

She slapped him hard across the face. The surprise was more jarring than the pain — though that was no picnic. He tried to shake free, but the thug tightened his grip. That hurt, too.

"Let him go," said Peshwar.

"Yeah!" said Luke, shaking out his arm dramatically once the man released it. "That's more like it." He turned to Peshwar. "So, what's next?"

She considered him silently and then said: "You run, little boy. That's what's next."

Luke looked into the black skull sockets that hid her eyes, and suddenly he understood. It took him a little longer than it would have taken most people, maybe, but now he got it. The others were gone. He was no use to The Order anymore. And with his cover blown, he never would be.

"This is your pay," said the lioness. "The chance to save yourself."

Without another word or another look, Luke spun around and sprinted across the valley floor. He'd had years of training and he did everything right: perfect posture, optimal stride length . . .

It didn't matter.

The valley floor in front of him lit up rose-red.

He lengthened his stride, leaning forward as if lunging for the finish line — and he was finished, all right. The energy dagger sank into his back with a dull crackling sound and a pain more intense than he'd ever imagined possible.

He fell to the hard desert ground, full-speed and face-first, like a gazelle gunned down midstride.

Evil thoughts flitted around Todtman, murderous urges so intense they almost seemed to have physical form. He fended them off as best he could, his hand on his amulet and the rubber tip of his cane punching the concrete floor of the warehouse as he moved briskly along one wall.

Somewhere beneath this massive building was The Order's headquarters. He was sure of it, but as he made his way through the shadowy space, he stopped short.

It wasn't a doorway or a guard that had caught his attention.

It was five massive blocks of stone, each nearly twice as tall as him and weighing tons. He examined the first of them. The surface was carved but weathered, thousands of years of sandy desert winds rounding the edges. And then, in one corner, he saw a more deliberate incursion.

The stone had been chipped away — *sculpted*. The shape emerging was unmistakable. A massive, muscular arm, as thick as a tree trunk, and at the end . . .

A hand, thought Todtman. *But such a hand*. A stone hand so large and strong that it looked as if it could control an entire world.

An evil thought slipped into his mind, whether from without or within, it was impossible to say: *That is exactly what this monstrous thing is being built to do.*

Don't Miss

TOMBQUEST™

BOOK 4
THE STONE WARRIORS

It's a race to find the Lost Spells!

If Alex and Ren are going to defeat the
Death Walkers for good, they have to find
the Lost Spells. The hunt takes them through
Egyptian tombs and an underground lair . . .
right to the stone warriors!

What purpose do these massive
warriors serve?

**Each book unlocks traps and treasure
in the TombQuest game!**

Log in now to join the adventure.
Scholastic.com/TombQuest

Enter your code to unlock traps and treasure!

RDP3GFT9XF